SILVER LINING

SKYE WARREN

CHAPTER ONE

ELIJAH

MY FATHER WAS the first man I killed.

He wasn't the last. Combat means seeing death up close and personal. I know the smell of death. The taste. The feel of it weighing down the air. It's heavy as hell.

Death turns the SUV I'm driving into a pressure cooker with me and Holly inside. Every bump on the road threatens to set us aflame. "You're going to be okay," I say, and my voice doesn't crack. I sound confident and sure. It's a fucking lie. "You're going to make it."

Plenty of times in my life, I've wished for death to slip a silent knife into my back.

Quicker that way. Cleaner. Easier.

Not now. Not when Holly is blinking in the passenger seat, her pretty brow furrowed as she looks down at the heart-colored stain spreading across her shirt. She doesn't know yet. Not on a conscious level. Adrenaline is flooding her body, shutting down higher thinking. She doesn't know one of the colonel's men shot her.

She doesn't know the bullet tore through soft flesh.

She doesn't know she's dying.

"Stay awake. Just stay the fuck awake. That's all you have to do." *Stay alive.*

The sound of the tires on pavement, the roar of the engine, they barely register as sound. Not after gunshots in the small, enclosed space of her apartment. I led her there from my abandoned-church-turned safehouse like a lamb to the slaughter. No, not exactly—I taught her how to shoot a gun before that. I left out the lesson about knowing the odds. Three armed enemies. One Holly. The math doesn't work.

She makes a sound that could be a question— *awake?* Then her head lolls onto her shoulder. She's passed out from the pain or the shock. Or sleeping. That's a nice thought. I can imagine her resting in the passenger seat instead of bleeding out.

The air gets heavier. Thicker.

I want to get out from under it. I want to breathe. But my lungs can't expand against the pressure and anyway there are things to do. We're two blocks from the church safehouse, where we should have stayed after I kidnapped her. Maybe forever.

Instead I have a limited amount of time to make a phone call.

None of my brothers will do any good right now. None of them can talk to me. That would only put them in danger. Yes, they're tough sons of bitches. Our father would have killed us if we weren't, but even they can't fight the whole of the United States government.

There'll be sirens soon, and when they stop, there will be other government operatives moving in the shadows. The person I need right now doesn't mind the darkness.

Dax answers on the second ring. "You better be on your knees with a firing squad behind you, if you're calling me. That's the only way I'm going to forgive you for going off the grid for two goddamn years. I thought you died. Or got married."

"I'm driving hot," I say between gritted teeth. "Heading toward the Meatpacking District. Got a friend with a GSW. Need medical assistance."

"It's the second one, isn't it? You got fucking leg shackled, didn't you?"

"If you want out, tell me now. I'm in real deep, and anyone near this will end up on a goddamn government watch list for the rest of their lives."

"I would be offended if I wasn't already on it."

Fair enough. Dax is part mercenary for hire, part arms dealer. That's the kind of company I kept before I met Holly, before I brought my brothers back into my life to protect her. For all this time, I tried to go straight. To do honest government contracts and security details. To be the man my brothers believe me to be.

That ended tonight.

I give him the address to the safe house. I've never given this information to another person, not even my brothers. His response is to hang up on me. He'll be here soon.

The church looms in the night, ominous and empty, a black hole in a shitty part of town. There are no lights as I kick the SUV over the curb and behind the building. It's mostly memory that guides me through the brick enclosure to the secure garage.

Steel doors slide open on well-oiled hinges.

Only when they close behind my tail lights can I finally take a deep breath.

You're going to be okay, I think, but I don't know whether I mean Holly or myself.

I gather up Holly's listless body out of the passenger seat. She's breathing. Such a faint movement. So fucking important. I cradle her head against my shoulder and carry her downstairs to a cot. I put a hand on her chin and shake. "Wake the fuck up."

She doesn't.

I head up the stairs for the first aid kit. One. Two. Three.

Around the corner, to the dusty office. Four. Five.

Six. Seven. Eight. Nine.

Nine seconds I leave her alone, and then I stop counting. There's work to be done if she has any hope of survival. She's exactly where I left her, arms curled up under her chin. I pull them away and rip her shirt in two, the fabric giving way to pure rage, exposing her pretty bra and the bloody wound on her side. I spill the first aid kit onto the foot of the cot and rip out sterile gauze. I'd clean the wound but there's too much blood. Have to stop the bleeding first. She groans when I press my big palms over the gauze and push hard.

Pressure. We need steady pressure. Her breathing is shallow, barely perceptible. And *I'm* only breathing through force of habit and circumstance. My habit is to keep exchanging oxygen and carbon dioxide even when I'm under enemy fire, and Holly is still alive.

For now.

More steady pressure. Her face is bone-white. The fire of her blood reaches my palms through the gauze. She needs an emergency surgical team, not battlefield first aid. I curse at the red liquid and focus my whole being on keeping what's left of her life in her body.

If she pulls through.

It won't just be murder. It will be treason. An electric urge moves through me and I ignore it. I can't move her now. Can't get her out of the country now, can't save her unless she lives. Can't do much of anything, except this.

I'm going to run out of gauze.

There's nothing else in the church aside from old wool carpet. Nothing up there is going to help me. Not the old prayers whispering in the ceiling. Not the abandoned pews.

And not God, if he's even there.

Dax arrives seven agonizing minutes later, one hand on the strap of a black backpack slung over his shoulder. He assesses the situation without flinching. That's why we're friends, me and Dax. He's seen the darkest shit this world has to offer, including a beautiful woman dying.

He drops the backpack to the cool stone floor. "Sitrep?"

"A single gunshot wound. One entry. One exit. I think it hit—" My throat clenches hard. A tiny piece of steel polymer ripped through her internal organs at a speed of two thousand feet per second. The fact that it went clean through is a good thing. It's a question of kinetic energy. Of physics, but it's not enough. "I think it hit her liver. She's not coughing blood."

She's barely breathing, but I don't say that out loud. He can see for himself.

He pulls his medical shit out of the backpack and drops things one by one in the empty spaces around Holly's body. Holly. Not her body. She's still inhabiting her body. It hasn't been abandoned yet. Dax checks her pulse. It's the neutral touch of a medical professional, and still, his fingertips against her skin make my teeth grind together. I'm like a wild animal backed into a corner. Only a matter of time before I bite.

Holly turns her head, her lips forming words that make no sound.

Dax is the one with the medical knowledge, but I've seen enough as a soldier. Enough to know that her odds are unknown right now. Incalculable. The bullet might as well have been a roulette ball around a wheel. It's a goddamn gamble. People get shot through the heart and live. They got shot through the liver and die. There's no logic to be found.

I have both palms splayed across the gauze, across Holly's side. My hands feel inadequate for the job set in front of me. Other jobs in my life have seemed bigger. Killing my father. Burying his body. But now those things are painfully, uselessly small.

They were nothing in comparison to this.

"I can't fix a bullet wound blind, Eli. Gonna have to move your hands." A sharp look in my direction. "Move your goddamn hands."

It's urgent. I know it is. It's a goddamn emergency. But how am I supposed to stay sane without my hands on her? Without being able to feel that she's warm and alive?

I give myself to the count of three, then gently lift my hands away.

Dax shoulders me out of the way, taking up all the space on the side of the cot. My bloodied hands hang uselessly at my sides. I should go wash them, but I can't. I'm stuck here, staring, past the event horizon of a black hole. Couldn't look away if I wanted to, and I don't want to. She doesn't react to the pinch of the needle. The goosebump sensation of superstition tiptoes up my back and grips me around the back of my neck. If I keep looking, she'll stay alive.

"I don't see a wedding band," he says, and it takes me a second to catch. The fight or flight response taking my body only allows for things like violence and fear.

"We aren't married."

"She say no?"

"I didn't ask her."

"What the fuck's taking you so long?"

What the fuck is taking me so long? Was I waiting for her to be shot? Was I waiting for her to bleed out in my arms? The reality is that I didn't have a life, didn't have freedom when I was beholden to the colonel. She knew that. That's why she shot him, to free me, but that's the thing. He owns me even in death. Lieutenant Colonel Mark Jefferson owns me for eternity. He'll take her away from me without drawing a single breath.

"Come here and clean this up."

Something hard untwists in the vicinity of my spine. Soldiers are men of action. They're not meant for standing around during battle. And this, for all it looks like a back alley operation, is a battle. Holly's fighting for her life. A fresh acid guilt burns through me. If it weren't for me, the colonel never would have come after her. She never would have fired that gun. She wouldn't be bleeding out on a safehouse cot in front of me.

My heart keeps beating while Dax stitches her up.

Holly's does too.

Dax has efficient hands. He's seen worse than this. So have I. I've caused things worse than this, but never to a civilian. Holly isn't a soldier and she shouldn't have been shot.

And none of this would have happened if I hadn't slipped a diamond into her bag years ago. There's no going back. Even if I could, I wouldn't.

That's the truth. The truth that digs in and hurts, even now. I wouldn't change a goddamn thing. I would still put that diamond in her bag, even if I knew she'd end up shot, even if I knew she'd end up kidnapped and hurt and dying in a church basement. I would still do every terrible thing if it meant knowing what she tastes like and what she feels like and what she sounds like.

Dax gives her a syringe of hardcore antibiotics.

There is no God in this church but there's a man with no qualms about operating outside a license. Close enough. A short eternity later he straightens over the cot, and it's only then that I notice the color returning to her cheeks.

Color.

Relief is a freight train. A tsunami wave. If I wasn't so used to standing up I'd fall to my knees, me, Elijah North, a trained killer and an aching, open wound.

Dax puts his fingers on Holly's neck, his brow furrowed, and takes stock of her pulse. Then he steps back from the table. For a horrifying instant I think he might pronounce the time of death, but instead he takes me by the arm and turns us away from the cots as if we're stepping outside of a real hospital room. My heart stays behind on that goddamn cot while Dax finds the bathroom and soaps up his hands.

He gives me instructions for the medicines he's leaving, as efficient and professional as any actual doctor. The information is so commonplace, like Holly's going to live and there'll be a future after all. "I'll handle it," I tell him, like I'm any other guy at a hospital bedside, waiting for the nurse to step out so he can take over.

Dax shakes his hands out over the sink and glances around. The bathroom is nothing fancy, nothing nice. It's half-abandoned, like the rest of the church. "New place?"

I glare at him.

"Watch your back," he says, because this is what he always says. The words unknot something at the pit of my gut. Holly deserves better than Dax, and better than me, but at least we have someone.

Back in the room, he slings his backpack onto his shoulder and steps out like he's just gotten word on his pager that it's time for rounds.

And I go to Holly's bedside. It's the only conceivable place for me to be in the world. My hand curls over hers before I know what I'm doing, before I can think about it.

A moment weighs itself down with silence broken only by her breathing. The rhythm is steadier now, but that doesn't mean she's healed. It doesn't mean she'll walk out of here okay. Nightmare scenarios line up and hurl themselves into my skull one by one, crowding in close, filling the room.

I must stay like that for hours. Maybe days. Time is meaningless without her.

She squeezes my hand. It startles me from my dark stupor.

I hold my breath, frozen, waiting. Her eyelids flutter, almost like she's dreaming, and then she opens them, blinking into the light.

Holly swallows once, twice, and licks her lips. The sight of the pink tip of her tongue on her bottom lip is more of a miracle than anything this church has ever seen. And when her eyes meet mine, I could almost believe there was something holy here once.

"Where am I?" Her thumb traces a lazy circle on the back of my hand.

"You're in hell, sweetheart. Welcome back."

CHAPTER TWO

HOLLY

SOME PEOPLE WISH they were mermaids. Some wish they weren't. But it's not the *being* that's the problem. It's the *becoming* that kills you. The transition, when flesh tears apart and reforms, when electricity runs through the invisible seams in your body. White-hot pain scorches me, and I twist my body in the fire. It might only last seconds or it might be an eternity in the roiling, beating, panting ache. The ache is relentless.

The pain becomes a constellation. Small pin-pricks of hurt in the black sky of my body. Hanging there with sharp metal pins that dig in and hold tight.

They're too far out of my reach to touch.

The stars turn to embers, sizzling at the dark fabric behind them. It's too late to put them out, and then all of them light up at once in a roar of fire and flame. A dragon—it must be a dragon.

It's as reasonable as becoming a mermaid, and I can feel him there, his hulking presence taking up all the space in my mind.

I can't get away. Can't move my legs, can't move my arms. You need muscles to sit up and mine won't engage. Even my own body won't save me from the danger. The threat is here. The threat is me. Somehow, I set this into motion, I thought this dragon into being, and now—

The dragon breathes again.

Fire consumes the stars and bleeds out into everything that's left of me.

It's a hot, obliterating pain, and sweat beads on my skin, on what remains of my skin. If I could open my mouth I would scream but the scream is burned away in a rush of wet heat. My body tries to get away, it tries so hard, but I'm too close to the dragon. I'd give anything for water. Cool water on my scales, on my legs, water to put it out, put it *out*.

I pray for the cool spray of the ocean. For rain.

Rain doesn't come.

Instead, I sink down into fire. A strangled animal noise comes from somewhere above me, beyond me, and it sounds familiar. Like my voice. But it can't be, because I don't have a voice anymore. I don't have anything but the pain.

The pain is everything. I'm nothing, nothing, nothing.

Nothing for a long time. Long enough that I hear a jagged drumbeat. The dragon's heart?

My heart.

It takes an eternity to think of *my heart*. My heart, which beats. My lungs, which draw air into my body. A new source of pain locates itself in my jaw. Well, that's what you get for gritting your teeth. In the still-dark of my mind I peek out the corner of my eye for signs of the dragon. No new flames light the space, only the hazy-red glow of the burned places.

The red gets brighter, and brighter, and brighter until finally I recognize the shade as light through my own eyelids. It adjusts itself off to the side of me.

Curiosity seeps in at the margins. A lamp to light someone's way? Maybe. Maybe not.

I'm sure I'm not moving. I'm sure now that I'm not a mermaid, not in the water, not even upright. Lying down. Lying back. How I got here is a mystery. Is this how a mermaid feels after she's made the change, the sand rough on her newly formed feet?

Fingers brush my chest, leaving trails of sparks

in their wake.

The room resolves into a familiar place. I recognize the bars and the walls, and most of all, the man with his head bowed over me, green eyes shadowed. He's tending to me. Working at something on my side. White gauze and sterile tape. Whatever he's doing hurts and an echo of the pain reminds me not to grit my teeth so hard.

"We keep meeting this way." His eyes flick up to my face, widening at my dry, raspy voice. Relief flashes there, but it's as quick as lightning. "In dark basements. Behind bars."

There's a sound in my throat. A soft whimper of recognition.

"Starting to feel like home, isn't it?" The corner of his mouth twists. "Or maybe that's just me. Maybe you wish you'd wake up somewhere else. Sorry about this next part."

What next part? Then he's doing something to raw flesh, and I sob at the newly cutting pain.

"Shh," he murmurs, sympathy thick in his voice. "I'll be quick."

I wish I could sink into the cot, but no matter how hard I press against it, it doesn't open up and swallow me whole. Maybe that dragon *was* real. Maybe it's breathing again, because sweat beads along my hairline and my eyes burn. A tear slips out along my teeth and now Elijah curses, his face dark with fury and guilt.

The expression he wears hurts almost as much as whatever he's doing. I have the strongest urge to look but I can't move my head, can't tip my chin down, don't want to see. Oh, he blames himself for this. It's written in every line of him. In his furrowed brow and the set of his shoulders and his teeth set tight together. His anger highlights the hard cut of his jaw. He's so gorgeous it hurts.

I want to reassure him, lift my hand to his cheek to follow the lines and curves there. Lifting my arm seems like too much work. Telling him I'll be fine would be an obvious lie. And besides, I'm not sure I could speak. I can't imagine how I could get up from this cot and walk away.

It's not so urgent, is it? Elijah doesn't seem to think so.

"Here," he says. "Drink some water."

There's no time to tell him no, that I can't, that the liquid would burn my cuts all the way down. There's already a glass at my lips. He tips it up, and water sluices down my throat. I gasp at the sensation. Tears sting my eyes.

"More." He's merciless.

I yank my head away, sending a splash of

water over my cheek, down my neck, curling at the nest of hair beneath me. It's biting cold against my overheated body. Ice against the sidewalk on a summer day in Paris—melting, melting. "No."

He wants to argue with me. I can sense that in the air, but he relents. Instead there's warm metal on my tongue. Salt. Broth. The soup goes down easier. I swallow, closing my eyes.

"Thank you," I whisper.

"Thank you," he repeats, his voice dry. Dry enough to be a desert. Dry enough to be the cracked skin across a large body covered in scales. "You're almost dead, and you're the one thanking me. Of course you are. That's our pattern. I get you killed, you thank me."

The words rush over me like a breath of too-hot air. They feel like fire. I know there's something in them I should argue, something I should protest, but the logic won't form in my mind. All I know is that I'm hurting, and so is he. We're both aching.

We're both becoming someone new.

"Are we in France?"

A quirk of his lips. He hasn't shaved. That's the only thing that registers. I want to run my fingers across his jaw to feel the bristles, the bite.

"No. We're far away from France."

I force the sounds past my swollen lips. "Italy?"

"No, sweetheart. We're a lot closer to home, and in more danger than we ever were overseas. Would that we were still in a French prison or in a gunfight through the Italian countryside. Those places would be infinitely safer than this."

My mind feels sluggish. Maybe it's the effects of the transition, flesh ripped apart and then sewed back together. Maybe this is what mermaids feel like when they're on land.

No. That's not right. I realize that now. I'm not a mermaid. That was a fever dream.

In reality I'm a woman, an ordinary woman, and this is Elijah. A soldier.

I tried to protect him. What hope did I have of that? Very little, but that didn't stop me. Love conquers all. That's what they teach you as a child. That's what my parents taught me, and it did feel as if their love could hold back the world. They didn't face bullets from the U.S. Army, I suppose. Love did nothing to block those.

"Sorry," I mumble, my tongue thick. The pain wants to drag me under, but I'm fighting it. This feels important, this moment with Elijah, his guilt like a phantom in the room.

I'm the one who shot the colonel. I'm the one who should suffer the consequences.

He gives a hard shake of his head. "No. Don't."

I'm not sorry I shot him. I'm only sorry I got hurt doing it. "Leave the country."

He gives me a look like I'm insane. "You wouldn't even survive the drive to the airport, sweetheart, much less a transatlantic flight."

"You."

Grief rips through his eyes. "And leave you here to—what? Die? Be arrested for treason? Fuck you for even suggesting that, sweetheart. No. Absolutely not."

"My fault."

Green is the most beautiful color. The color of dragons. Those green eyes watch me with a possessive gaze, as if I'm made of pure gold. "It's my fault for letting that man within six feet of you. My fault for not killing him years ago. You were a warrior in there."

"What will we do?"

Uncertainty. It's only there for a flash. Half a second and then it's gone. In its place there's the determination that I'm used to seeing, but it's too late. I've already seen beneath his armor. He doesn't know how to protect us anymore. "No one knows we're here."

"You own?" Does he own the church?

A huff of humorless laughter. "Ironic, isn't it? A man like me owning the church. You'd think it would have gone up in flames the moment I signed the papers. Just more proof that there's no god anywhere to be found in those pews."

He forces more of the broth down my throat until I pull my head back again. This time it's warm, salty soup that runs down my throat to pool at the hollow there.

His gaze is fierce, his touch gentle as he wipes me up. "No one knows I own this place. It's buried under layers of shell corporations. It won't be easy to uncover."

Not easy but not impossible. And the U.S. government will have resources the average person does not. That means we're sitting in an hourglass, each grain of sand falling, leading closer and closer to the time when we're discovered.

What happens then? Nothing good.

"Your brothers."

"I'm not involving them. This goes beyond what North Security can handle. Even sharing their last name is enough to get them questioned at this point."

"They would want to help you." The words

come out hoarse, because I want to help him. The same way I tried to help my sister on that urgent plane ride to Paris. Clumsily, armed only with a sense of right and wrong, with a love not strong enough to block bullets.

He swallows hard. "It doesn't matter what they want."

Those are the words he says, but what I hear is, *It doesn't matter what I want.* Everyone wants their family. Even someone from a dark past full of abuse like him. He's alone.

That's when I realize I'm alone, too.

Even if I manage to heal enough to stand up, to walk out of this church, I'll never be able to go back to my family, not with this murder on my hands. It would be too dangerous for them. They would be harboring a fugitive. I'll never see London again. Never see my mom or my dad again. A tear slips down my cheek, following the trail of cooled broth.

Pain detaches itself from the space under his hands and curls lower to rest on my belly. Not as heavy down there. When it settles, I can bear it.

My eyelids are heavy, though, heavier by the minute.

Sleep feels cool, like the water I craved. I still crave it, but my lips won't form the words. I'll drink later. There will be a later, at least.

The pressure lifts off the wound and tension runs out of my body like rain. A careful hand brushes a lock of hair away from my forehead and smooths it down.

That's the last thing I feel before my head slips under the surface.

CHAPTER THREE

LONDON

THESE STAIRS ARE going to kill me.

I know, I know. The cocaine addiction will probably get me in the end. But the three flights to my walkup in Red Hook are giving the coke a run for its money. At least the stairs get my heart pumping and fresh oxygen into my blood. A girl needs to be revitalized after an endless day ringing up bougie coffee orders and having her face blasted by the moisture from a steam wand. The scent of espresso drifts off my clothes as I make the third-floor landing. The scent of coffee grounds follows me even into my dreams. Hazard of the job.

The key sticks in the lock and I force it, mapping out the path to the shower. Kick my shoes off at the door. Shirt off by the time I'm through the postage-stamp living room with my ratty couch.

Do not pass go, do not get dinner, do not do

anything but climb into the water and stand there as long as it's hot. I kick off my shoes, drop my purse, and step into the living room.

I'm reaching for the hem of my shirt when I see it, see *him*, and freeze.

The couch isn't empty.

There's a dead body on it.

I should run screaming in the other direction. I should call the cops, sobbing and hysterical. Part of me knows this, but the bigger part of me is… curious. It's always been my downfall.

A step closer. And another. The large mass of muscled man compiles into someone I know. It's Adam Black. The man who kidnapped my sister.

The man who saved her, too.

My heart crawls up into my throat. What is he doing here, in my apartment? I know I locked the door when I left. Did he manage to pick the lock in this condition? With that much blood on his shirt, he didn't fight his way in here.

I don't have time to consider the implications of the still-intact lock on the door, not really. Not when there's a dead man on my couch. A cold flash freezes the back of my neck, followed by a hot flush of panic. Smuggling diamonds is one thing. Dealing with a dead body is another. The police are out of the question for a man like

Adam. For a woman like me.

My pulse slams against my eardrums, working overtime, and I take a deep breath. It does nothing to crack open the icy fear encasing my lungs. *Think of him as a man asleep on a couch, London. One step closer. One more. There.*

From this vantage point—hovering over him, a half-step from the couch—things look even worse. His shirt has caved in to the wound below it. The fabric is soaked in blood. Adam has his face turned toward the back of the couch and he looks so still, so horribly still.

A bruise paints one of his cheeks.

I reach for him before I know what I'm doing. Oh, god. What if he's cold?

If he's cold, it's too late, it's way too late. I'm going to have to walk out of this apartment and never come back, not ever. I'll have to convince Holly not to look for me, and she won't be convinced. I know she won't.

My fingertips are a whisper away from the purple bruise when he moves, a hand shooting out to grab my wrist. I suck a huge breath in for a scream and then swallow the sound, jagged edges and all. My pulse is too big for my veins, the silvery burst of adrenaline so powerful it feels like an electric shock. His eyes meet mine with sharp focus.

"Who did this to you?" My voice sounds thin and high and I swallow that, too. No time for falling apart now. "Who hurt you?"

His pupils recede, and he lets his head fall back on the one throw pillow I own. "An old friend."

My mouth has gone dry, but I manage a casual tone. "With friends like that, who needs enemies?"

He huffs his amusement, focus slipping away from me and onto the ceiling. "I have enemies, too. Believe me, they're worse."

I detach his hand from my wrist and run my fingers through my hair. "Jesus. Okay. You're here in my apartment. And you're hurt, you're dying, you're—"

"Shot." He winces as he pushes himself up against the arm of the couch. Not upright, but inclined. I can tell he pays a cost for this. "You can look, if you're interested."

"If I'm *interested*." My lips buzz with a new bolt of adrenaline. What else is there to do but lift his shirt away from the wound? We both fumble with the project until the formerly gray fabric is over Adam's head. There's more blood underneath. Too much to see what I'm doing. "I'm going to help you, but first I need to freak the fuck out. Wait here."

"No, I've got to go. I've got an important meeting." A wry smile curves his lips, but he lays his head back on the arm of the couch and clenches his jaw.

I soak a clean towel through with hot water, studiously ignoring my shaking hands. And then I return to where Adam's breathing fast and shallow on the couch, the bloodied t-shirt clenched in one fist. He lets out a breath when I perch on the couch next to him, and another one when I touch the towel to his skin. "Be quick about it," he says, his teeth gritted.

When the worst of the blood has laid claim to the towel I can see the wound.

Small. Raw. Circular. A bullet wound. I thought my heart couldn't beat faster, but it does. "You need a hospital. I'm not a doctor. I don't even play one on TV. This is ridiculous."

"No fucking hospitals." His eyes go black with this, spearing through mine.

"You're delirious. You're drunk on pain and probably blood loss."

"I'm stone-cold sober."

I fold the sacrificed towel up and toss it toward the kitchen. "I don't know how to treat a gunshot wound, Adam. What am I supposed to do? Put a Band-Aid on it?"

His eyes do that thing again, sliding away from my face to some distant point behind me, and a cold point of fear pricks at my gut. His lips curl in amusement. "Google it."

"That's not funny."

The shake in my voice seems to sober him. "No. It's not funny. I'll need tweezers. And towels. Lots of them. More than that scrap you had before. All the towels you own, probably."

"I hope this part is a joke."

He narrows his eyes. "And alcohol."

"To clean the wound?"

"No, to drink. This is going to hurt like a motherfucker."

Not a joke. Not a joke at all. This has passed a new threshold for serious situations in my life. A man is literally dying on my couch. I'm the only one here to save him.

"*Now*," prompts Adam, and up and moving again. Tweezers are in the bathroom. All of my clean towels are shoved into one rickety closet, and the closet won't give them up. It's like the closet wants him to die. Fuck the closet. That's not happening tonight, not if I can help it. And I'm going to have to help it. There's nobody else.

In the kitchen I pull down a single fifth of vodka from the cupboard over the fridge. It's never been opened. The top refuses to give, my fingers slippery around the ridges, until I take a deep breath and force it.

Back in the living room, Adam has dropped the t-shirt and has one hand pressed next to the wound. Not on top of it, but close, as if he can't bear to touch it. He takes the vodka with his free hand and drinks and drinks and drinks until I'm forced to think about stopping him. How much alcohol is too much when you're trying to save yourself from a gunshot wound?

The bottle's half gone when he puts it down on the floor and holds his hand out for the tweezers.

I take a deep breath. "Are you sure—"

He snaps his fingers, and I drop them into his open palm.

Adam doesn't hesitate. For a guy who's just downed too much vodka, he's surprisingly deft as he flips them into his fingers and digs them into the wound. My entire body freezes, watching this. Watching the serious lines in his face get overtaken by the pain. His teeth catch his lower lip and press down hard. My heart goes wild with how useless I am, with how raw this is, and I'm going to explode. I'm on the verge of begging him to stop when he gives the tweezers a sharp yank.

A bullet dangles from the end of them. Adam holds it up in front of his face. Inspecting it? Reassuring himself that it's out? His eyes roll back in his head and he's out before I can ask.

I put a hand on his shoulder and rub. "Adam."

No answer.

I check his pulse. It's still there.

"This is really not funny," I tell him, and he doesn't respond with so much as a twitch of his eyelids. Because now I *do* have to Google how to wash and bandage the wound. What the fuck was he going to do with the towels? I can't just dry off the blood and hope it seals itself up.

I open up a private browser on my phone and type in the search.

Keep the wound clean and dry. Wash with clean water twice per day.

Apply Vaseline to the wound. Cover with clean bandage or other cloth.

Jesus. I have Vaseline, I think, but if I need bandages I'll have to run down to the store. And I should do it soon, before the wound bleeds anymore or gets infected because all I could come up with was a ratty t-shirt ripped into strips.

I take my last bottle of water out of the fridge and use it to wash out the bullet hole while he's still unconscious. It seems like the smart thing to do, even if the Google search result didn't explicitly say so.

And then I check the living room window.

Nothing looks too suspicious down on the street. No lurking figures or white vans. Still, my heartbeat gets faster, louder. "The NSA definitely tracked that search," I murmur to my reflection in the window. "I hope this was worth it." *I hope you were worth it, Adam.*

My reflection has no answer for that.

CHAPTER FOUR

ELIJAH

MUFFLED KEYSTROKES ON the other end of the phone line punctuate a distracted silence.

"Howie."

Silence. I shift in a pew five rows back from the front and watch the last of the sunset fade through the last of the stained glass. Not all of the original windows have survived over the years. I've had them replaced with plain, clear glass. Now that I have time to look at them, I'm regretting the decision. It would at least be more interesting to look at while I wait for Howie to come out of his trance.

He is probably the last person on earth named Howard. The nickname might be a joke, come to think of it. You never know with hackers.

"I don't believe your name is Howard," I say.

There's a sharp rustle, like plastic wrap up against his speaker. "What?"

"Are you going to update me or not?"

"I was checking up on our happy couple. They're all settled in at the resort. Nothing new to report there. The rental car was checked in a couple of hours ago, and I'm still waiting to see—"

He takes me through the list of red herrings. Sooner or later, the Army's going to realize they're all false leads, but for now they'll be busy. We sent a couple matching our description on an all-expenses-paid trip to the Bahamas. We paid another guy to rent a car with a planted alias and drive it across the country. Three separate women have checked into mid-tier roadside motels at various locations. There are others. There will be more if necessary.

For now, Holly is safe with me in the abandoned church.

Howie has started typing again, and his words tumble out with increasing speed until he reaches the end of his updates. "Gotta go."

He doesn't wait for me to answer before he ends the call.

I stand up from the pew and stretch, my ass aching from the unforgiving curve of the wood. I should've ripped out all of these cursed benches when I bought the church. It makes a kind of poetic sense, though, that the pews are straight out of hell.

Worship should be uncomfortable. At least the kind that was done here.

Eventually the Army will break through the paper trail obscured by the shell corporations, but for now this place is safe. Holly needs to rest if she has any hope of recovering.

I take the stairs back down to the basement. Being here with her has attuned me to every small sound in the building, which is how I know she's already awake. I hear her movement before it should be possible and pick up the pace. Go through the door.

Find her sitting up on one of the cots, rubbing at her eyes with the back of one hand. I'm across in a matter of steps, one arm around her, easing her back down to the pillow.

Holly glares at me all the way down, her protest lighting her face, but I can see from the tightness around her eyes that it cost her. That little show of strength, sitting up in bed, it cost her.

I stroke her hair away from her face. "You need to rest."

"That's all I've been doing for the past year." Her voice is sweet gravel laced in pain. It's hard to stay awake with painkillers like she's on. The stubborn set of her jaw is proof that lying around is not Holly's favorite thing. "Lying down. Staying low. Hiding."

"It's been three days since you were shot."

"Well, it feels like longer. Especially with no windows." Holly turns her head into the palm of my hand. It's a fleeting closeness. It hurts her to turn over, so she doesn't. She stops herself, except when she's dreaming. The glancing touch of her warm skin on mine is enough to set me on fire. No, I'm not a good man. I'm definitely not, if I'm lusting after an injured woman.

A narrow table, more of a cart on legs, holds all the supplies I need to change the dressing on her wound. This is all I do. I bring Holly glasses of water. I press pills onto her tongue and make her swallow. I come back again and again with soup and clean blankets and more bandages and gauze. It's as painful as sitting on the goddamn pew upstairs. More painful.

The guilt is a sickness all its own, and it's eating me alive.

I had Dax bring me clothes for her, and I reach for a fresh shirt.

She watches me with her brown eyes clouded with the pain she tries to hide. It hurts when I touch her this way, and I have spent every waking hour trying to make it better and failing. The guilt never sleeps. It balls itself up in the back of my throat and chokes me.

"We'll take you somewhere with windows next," I tell her while I peel away the old gauze as gently as humanly possible. There never would have been time for this kind of care on the battlefield. On any battlefield.

And we're in a battle now, albeit a quieter one. Every minute that we're here, I want to leave. I want to run. But there's no running to be done now. She has to heal.

"Maybe somewhere with no walls. You can go hiking and sleep under the stars."

Holly gives me a hazy smile, like light through those stained-glass windows if the windows were the color of hurt. "You and me, both. Do you promise?"

"Yes." It's a lie.

We're being hunted by the U.S. government like animals. If they find this place, if they chew through all the layers of shell companies and anonymous purchases and frantic drives from her apartment to the basement of one abandoned church, then we'll be caught. And if we're caught, the catching will be the least of our worries. We'll be tortured. Probably executed.

I haven't said any of this to Holly. How would it help to know, even though it's true?

And the other truth, underpinning the constant prickling at the base of my spine:

It's inevitable.

The government has time and money and manpower to tie up all our loose ends. A wild goose chase won't keep them running forever. They will find us. Maybe not today, but someday.

There is no happy ending for us.

I thought I was used to the prospect of a bleak future. Enough nights down in a well will teach you not to expect much from a new dawn. With Holly, knowing the outcome is a thousand times harder than a steep climb out of dark water.

In some ways, the well would be easier. At least back then I was down there alone.

Holly's gritting her teeth and trying to hide it when I'm finished with the dressing. Her body fails to hide all its trembles and shakes while I button her shirt. I don't know who she thinks she's fooling, but it's not me. Fresh guilt slices its way through my ribs and into soft guts. Water. Pills. I help her with both, and as soon as she swallows her muscles relax. They don't work that fast, but a person can anticipate relief as powerfully as they can anticipate pain.

I pull up the sheet and smooth it over her, careful not to brush the dressing, hiding it beneath layers of cloth. Protecting it, as much as it can be protected. Her tongue darts out to wet her lip and she lets out a sigh. Holly watches the ceiling like a screen in a drive-in movie. They're going sweetly unfocused. She's starting to fall asleep. I'm relieved. I'm relieved, and I shouldn't be.

I shouldn't wish for her to be silent and far away. But being awake hurts her.

Seeing her in pain hurts me.

"What would it be like?"

I brush my knuckles over her cheek. How is she still so soft, after everything?

"Stars," I tell her, and the scene springs to life in front of me. The church basement and the cot with its white sheets dissolve into a humming dark. "There would be a million stars to look at. Skies so clear we could lie there and watch the constellations rise and set. We'd bring blankets and lay them out to watch. It would be warm if we held onto each other."

Holly's eyes flutter closed. The corner of her mouth curls in a smile. "Keep going."

"We'd find a brook to drink from. Or maybe a lake, the kind that appears so suddenly. One minute there's grass and ground. The next there's water filled with reeds. They'd wave above the water while we slept. Or while we didn't sleep."

She laughs, the sound as dreamy as her eyes. Holly leans into my touch, her cheek warm against my palm. Blissfully warm. Heat means she's alive. I haven't stopped touching her, but I should.

I can't.

"The ripples move through the reeds and onto the grass. They're steady. And calm, for our camping trip. Calm water. The same sound wakes us up in the morning with the sun. Time means nothing out there. Everyone has enough."

I don't know what I'm saying anymore, but I keep talking. There are enough words to describe a day on the shore of the lake. A swim. An afternoon in the shade of a tent. An evening with a blazing sunset over the reeds and the water. Food over a campfire. Hot dogs and marshmallows. Innocent things. Things that make people like Holly happy. Stars, infinite stars.

Her breathing evens out. Gets deeper. I still can't pull my hand away from her face. Not for a long time. The sunset is long over outside the church by the time I stand up and go about the second set of tasks. Getting rid of old gauze.

Setting out new supplies. Counting her pills. We have enough water. There's enough food. I turn off the overhead light and turn on an antique lamp brought down from the old church office.

It's only when I take my seat again and listen to Holly's deep breathing that I realize—

I wasn't describing some fictional campground.

I was describing the woods in France where I fucked her for the first time. That's my definition of peace. That's the place I'd go back to if I could.

CHAPTER FIVE

HOLLY

MY SIDE THROBS.

It throbs constantly, like those damned ripples Elijah put into my brain. I don't know how he got them there, only that he did, and now it's all I can think about. My body is a lake. The pain ripples through me, through the reeds. They get smaller with the painkillers and larger when the painkillers wear off but they are always, always there.

Living in this church is driving me insane.

But the pain is the worst of all.

Sometimes, the painkillers don't touch it. They leave it whole. During those times I can't move. My strongest instinct is to stay still, because if I stay still, then it can't dig its claws in deeper.

It would be easier if I weren't so tired of lying down.

I'm either unconscious or I'm hurting.

I am bone-tired of being here, on this cot. So

tired that the exhaustion comes full circle and I'm wide awake, pointing my toes to stretch, trying to bend my knees. Anything. Anything other than lying still. Sometimes, I try to get up.

And Elijah stops me.

It feels like I'm still in France in that medieval church. Like I never really escaped. Like the last six months of my life have been a dream I created in my madness.

Sometimes I try to get up, but he is always here, urging me back down onto the cot.

I know he's going to do it. I know he'll rush in here the moment I so much as breathe deeply, but I can't help it. I need to move. And so I try again, holding my breath while I push myself up on one elbow. Trying to be as silent as possible.

It doesn't matter.

Elijah must have been waiting outside the door because he steps in before I'm fully upright. This time, when I grit my teeth, it's to keep in the frothing resentment expanding in my veins. In this moment I resent all of him. All of his carved good looks and determined green eyes and gentle hands. Even his sympathetic expression.

Especially his sympathetic expression.

"You need to rest." He eases me back down on the pillow for the millionth time, his tone infuriatingly even. As if I'm a child and he's my parent.

"I'll go insane if I rest for another minute." I can feel the insanity creeping in at the borders of my body. It's a buzzing in my elbows and my shoulders and down by my hips. "I mean it."

He sighs, dropping into the seat next to the cot. Most times when I wake up, he's there. He's always there.

"Your body needs more time."

"And then what? When this is gone, will I still be trapped here in the church?" I gesture to the wound at my side, the movement causing a twinge of pain through the skin and muscle. I don't allow my face to react. The sports bra was a fun development in the wound-healing process. I go shirtless now, with no bandages, so my skin can knit itself back together in the open air.

The wound itself looks small now. Only an inch and a half of red scar tissue. Ironically it hurts now more than ever. On the inside, it feels like knives. I ignore the sharp points and keep looking into Elijah's eyes. He's going to answer me, damn it.

He shifts in his chair. "No."

"You're lying to me. We're stuck here, aren't we? Because of me. Because I shot him." For the rest of my life, I'll remember the sensation of recoil. It was different than when Elijah taught me to shoot. The bullet seemed to weigh more, even hanging in the air, even separate from me.

"Don't worry about that right now."

My heart beats harder, forcing more blood through my veins. My head throbs along with my wounded side. It takes a real effort not to grind my teeth together until they crack. How can he be so consistently calm about all of this? I'm ready to shed my skin like a snake and disappear into a puff of smoke, and there Elijah sits, watching me with concern in his eyes. I hate it.

"I did it to free you. So you could finally be rid of him."

He looks away. "And you succeeded."

"Except now I'm wanted for murder."

"No one knows what happened in that apartment."

"The men with him definitely know what happened. They shot me."

"You don't need to worry about them any-more."

I'm not worried, precisely. It's more like I'm in eternal agony. I know I'm losing perspective, but it doesn't feel like I'll ever really heal. If I live ten more years, or twenty, there will still be this terrible pain in my side. It's as if I really was a mermaid who turned into a human. Now I forever have to walk the sandy shore, unsteady and excluded, in this new form.

He's giving me that patient look again.

"You should be angry," I say, venom in my voice. I'm the one angry—at circumstances, at the pain. And some of that anger transfers to the only other human I've seen in weeks. "You should be furious at me for pulling the trigger. For killing a man."

"I've killed more men than you will ever know."

"For killing *that* man. Your mentor. Your commanding officer."

"He was a bastard. I once watched him order a man under his command to eat peanuts, knowing he was allergic to them. One. Two. Three. He ate them until he went into shock. He died, Holly. That's who you stopped. Someone who killed for the joy of it."

That makes me shiver. The colonel wasn't a good man, but hearing that story makes him more real. As if his ghost haunts this old church now, malevolent and cold. "You shouldn't make excuses for me. It's because of me that you're hiding right now."

He runs a hand over his face, and I see a crack in the facade. He's exhausted, and I know I'm to blame for that. He's hurting, only his wounds don't bleed like mine. "What do you want me to say? That I'm glad he's dead? I am. That you shouldn't have killed him? No, that was my fucking job. I failed you."

"Hate me," I say, and he's already shaking his head before the words are out.

"You were protecting me. No one has ever done that before. Even my brothers—I don't blame them. They saved themselves the only way they knew how, but they didn't save me. No, I did that the day I killed my own father. No one has ever protected me before you."

I force myself upright—yes, finally—and Elijah puts up his hands to stop me. I throw all of my frustration into my glare, and he stops, putting his hands back into his lap. I hate that even more than I hate his calm, his composure. Fighting him would be better than this. I'd fight him right now if he tried to stop me again. Even if it meant tearing open the wound. Damn it, I wish he would, but of course he doesn't give me the satisfaction. Only a patient look.

"I'm tired of this." There's a broken edge to my voice that I also hate. So much hate and pain that I'm drowning in it. It tastes metallic on my tongue. "Of you taking care of me. Of being an invalid. Of having you take care of me like a goddamn martyr."

His green eyes turn dark, the color of moss in a forest. "I'm a shit caregiver. I know that."

"It's exactly the opposite. You're perfect. Too damned perfect. I want you to rail at me. Yell, scream, tell me you're sick and tired of feeding me chicken broth, because I'm damn sure tired of eating it." I'm too loud, the rising voice too much for my overtaxed body, but I don't care. I don't care. I can't care any longer.

Elijah's lip quirks. "You want Chinese take-out?"

"Yes. But I can't have it. We'd be found out." I know this like I know he'll come in here at the first sign I've tried to move. I know this like I know the edge of guilt in his eyes that never leaves. It's there when I wake up, and there when I fall asleep, just like the relentless pain.

"I can maybe sneak a dumpling or two." It's a joke. A gentle joke for the woman who's slowly going insane in the basement of a church. Elijah runs a soothing hand over my arm, a gentle pressure reminding me—yet again—that I need to rest.

He lets the silence settle over us like a blanket. I could kill him for being so perfect. I could kill him and kiss him and fight him if he'd just let me.

All my anger seeps into the ceiling and taunts me from up there, as useless as I am. I'm reduced to a hand on my arm. It's not the kind of touch I crave from Elijah. It's so neutral and bloodless that I don't recognize it at all, never mind that it's the way he's been touching me for days.

I don't know this man. This perfect, steady man who never shows me anything but competent concern. He's been like some kind of caring robot, never flinching at my pain or at the blood, never losing his patience.

What happened to the beast who bared his teeth behind bars?

I've been trapped in this cell with the prince instead. A stranger.

CHAPTER SIX

ELIJAH

S HE'S PUSHING ME.

Holly doesn't lay back down. She tips her head back and glares at the ceiling.

That's good.

Because I can't let her see. I can't let her see how close they are to the surface—my guilt, my shame. The violence that sits at my core. It wouldn't take much to bring them out into the open. It never has taken much, and they're like monsters now. They chew at the marrow of my bones and threaten to burst out of my flesh.

Her breathing is uneven now, hitched and angry. How could I not react to her? It's been abject misery, tending to her without having her. The misery is almost powerful enough to override the aching lust at the core of me. Goddamn it, I want her. I want so much from her that I can't have. Too much from her. I've taken too much already.

I let my hands ball into fists and release them.

I don't want to hurt Holly.

I *can't* hurt her.

She's already injured. She was shot trying to save me from an inevitable fate. Does she realize how much this eats at me? By the end of all this, I'll be nothing but a flayed heart. I'd rather take a hundred bullets than mar her smooth skin.

Memory intrudes, shouldering its way past weakened defenses. In that apartment I wasn't a man anymore. I wasn't a soldier.

I was a child, three years old, watching my mother die in front of my eyes. I couldn't save her then. I can't save Holly now. The bullet wound might be healing but the threat that looms outside these walls can't be stopped. It can't ever be stopped.

Holly shifts closer to the edge of the cot, and my hands come up. Force of habit. I stop myself from touching her at the last moment as she eases herself onto the floor. "Don't do this."

"Don't do what?" Her legs tremble with the effort of standing, and there's high color in her cheeks, pain she tries to hide, but it's so clear. It's sketched all over her brown eyes like lightning across a dark sky. "Don't move? Don't talk? Don't be a person?"

"Don't hurt yourself." It's not often that I feel even an echo of desperation. I learned not to feel that a long time ago. But I feel it now, like a distant wave.

"You're hurting me," she whispers, and my heart clenches. Stops. Starts again.

I don't know how to tell her that we won't survive.

The right combination of words will never come. We're sinking, drowning, and I'm going to smile and nod and reassure her all the way to the goddamn ocean floor. I'm not going to tell her that we'll probably die. "I never said I knew how to love."

Her eyes flash, surprise in the lift of her eyebrows. "You love me?"

"Why the fuck do you think I'm pushing you away?" This hurts more than the guilt and the shame. It's an awful, tearing truth and it feels like sandpaper leaving my lips. It feels like fire in the lungs and steel through my gut.

"I thought it might be the other thing." Both corners of her mouth turn down, vulnerability flickering through her expression and disappearing.

"Hate?" Every muscle reaches for her. Longs for her. My palms ache. "Yes, I think I hate you too. For making me want you. For making me weak. And most of all, I hate you for putting yourself in danger."

Holly takes a quick step forward, too fast, and the hate detonates into fear. I grab for her without thinking and pull her between my legs. She gasps.

"That hurt." She steadies herself with her small hands on my shoulders, and I'll be damned, I'll be fucked. She sounds wondering. Relieved. Not like I've just done the unthinkable and kicked her when she was down. "Finally."

"Finally? *Finally?*" I'm so pissed at her, so righteously enraged, that I do the only thing I can think to do and wrestle her into a kiss. Damn her for being so reckless. Damn me for putting her in a scrap of cloth that's barely a bra so I can see her peaked nipples pushing up the fabric. Damn us both to another circle of hell.

Holly kisses me back hard, groaning into my mouth. I have to be killing her.

I stand her up again, trying to push her away, but she digs her nails into the backs of my hands. "No," she says. "No." Then she reaches for me again.

"I'm hurting you."

"Yes." She follows this with a bite and I bite her back, then soothe the bite with my tongue.

It's been torture, not kissing her. Not taking her mouth. Not taking her. I've taught her plenty of lessons about the way she should behave, the way she should not fucking push me, and she hasn't learned a single one.

With the taste of her on my lips my restraint shatters. It's been weak for days. Weak since I brought her down to this crypt knowing that we were never coming out alive. I have felt every second pass us by. All of them. Ticking down to the moment when death takes us and wishing I could do this to pass the time.

I sink my teeth into the flesh of her shoulder and this time the noise she makes is so dirty, so filthy, that I do it again just to hear it. "The fuck is wrong with you?" I murmur into her skin.

"You're what's wrong with me." She rakes her nails under the collar of my shirt. Four bright lines against my skin. I hope she scars me. I hope I never stop feeling her touch, not until I draw my last breath. "Hate me even more, sweetheart. Make me feel it."

"I hate you so fucking much."

"More than that." I try to catch her by the wrist but she's determined to get to my pants.

Which she does.

To my belt and my zipper, and then she's

fumbling with the waistband.

Damn us both.

I help her.

I help her because I don't want her to move any more than she has to. At least that's the excuse I give myself. There's no good reason to be pulling out my erect cock when she's injured. It's a dangerous game with open wounds. Get too carried away and they'll reopen.

If she's not careful, she'll do real damage, and all the time I've spent keeping her in that goddamn bed will have been for nothing.

The truth is I help her because I want her too much to stop. I need her too much.

If this is the end, and it is, then I'm not shuffling off the goddamn mortal coil without having her one more time. I'm already so hard it hurts when Holly swirls one finger around my tip.

This should be slow and gentle. I should hold my breath and try not to touch her. She should be ready to tap out when it gets to be too much, and it will get to be too much. Sex is always too much when you're recovering from a bullet wound.

I can't love her that way.

Not now.

Not ever.

Holly's eyes light up when I pin her wrist in a

firm grip and guide her closer. "Don't fuck around," I warn her. "Not unless you want to suffer the consequences."

She bites at her lip. "I do want that. I thought it was obvious."

Fine. Never mind the bullet wound, never mind fucking anything. An animal surge of adrenaline and need pulls my muscles tight. I'm dying of the need to fuck. Worse than that. To rut.

I'm an animal right now, and Holly doesn't mind.

She sighs with what sounds like relief when I shove down her pants. Her panties. I kick them as far away from us as I can get them, and then I pull her into my lap. Spread her thighs wide. And notch the tip of me to the core of her, where she is very, very wet.

Goddamn it, she's slick and hot and tight, and the minute I touch her there, I'm lost.

I fuck into her like she's not hurt. Like we're in those woods in France. Like the worst of everything is still ahead of us. Holly sinks down onto me with a hiss, hands braced tight on my shoulders, and I would take a thousand bullets to keep feeling the sweet grip of her pussy every minute for the rest of my goddamn life.

If I feel it another second now, this will be over.

I won't have that.

It's torture to lift her off me and onto the cot. It feels like hell. Holly protests, fighting me when I shove the pillow under her head and fighting me when I push her down on the bed.

It takes a lick between her legs to settle her down. To shock her into some semblance of submission. It's not enough for me, fuck, it will never be enough, but a long lick makes her shiver and clench.

She digs her fists into the sheets and rocks her hips up to my face.

It's twisted, how hot it makes her to be fucked rough. It's twisted and it makes her dangerous to me and more dangerous to herself.

And it doesn't matter anymore.

We're a runaway train and we won't survive the crash, but I'll die with the taste of her on my tongue.

Holly calls me a bastard when I tease her hole. She calls me worse when I find her clit and worry at it with my teeth. She keeps saying something, over and over again, her voice so breathy and senseless that I don't know what the hell she means until she gets a grip on the words:

Why did you stop, why did you stop?

Stop what?

Stop fucking her.

I told her I don't know how to love her, but the truth is that I do. I know exactly what she wants. I shouldn't give it to her. For a man like me, wrestling with the brutal morality of this is an exercise in shame and lust. Jesus, who wants to hurt a woman the way I want to hurt Holly? What kind of man would want that?

The kind of man I am.

I want it so much that my skin feels too tight. I want it so much that I'm devouring her for the sole purpose of making it last longer for me. She's right. I am a bastard. An asshole. The devil himself.

I lift myself up to kiss one of her hip bones. Once I'm there I bite her too. "I'll hurt you," I tell the bite mark. "I'll take it too far. You need to rest. You need—"

Her fingers twist in my hair. Holly shouldn't have the strength to bring me up over her but she does. "If you say that I need to rest one more time—"

"What, you'll run away? You won't get far."

"I'll die," she promises, and a strange light in her eyes tells me it's true. Maybe the truest thing she's ever said. Her hips buck up into the air, fucking into empty air.

It has to be killing her.

And here she is, telling me that she'll die without my dick.

A desperate joy bursts like a firework in my chest. She wants me. She wants me so much she can't stop her hips from moving. She can't stop her hands from digging into my shirt. She is still, even now, making small noises in the back of her throat that tear down every bit of my reserve.

There's none left.

It's gone.

"I'll die without this," she says again, and I believe her.

CHAPTER SEVEN

HOLLY

I DON'T THINK Elijah knows how hard his fist is punching into the flimsy cot.

He doesn't know, he can't know, what he looks like right now—like all of him is barely contained in his body. I'm witnessing a one-man brawl. I *caused* a one-man brawl.

I needed it.

Still do.

He doesn't know what he looks like but I know what I must look like. Needy. Wild with it. Hungry for all the dirty things that you're not supposed to want out of a man.

I admit it. I *am* needy. I need for him to look this way, with his glittering eyes and gritted teeth. I need for him to see me as a woman and not some wounded creature to be pitied and tended and soothed. Not some pathetic person to be spoken to with extreme patience at all times.

I need him to fuck me.

More. Again. Despite everything. If I'm going to be trapped forever in a medieval basement with Elijah then I want something out of it, damn it, I want him.

My last painkillers are wearing off. They burn away into a clarity that reminds me of a sunrise over water. It paints everything in vivid colors and sharp detail.

His eyes. His hands. The hitched rise and fall of his breath.

Elijah's standing there in a tangle of pants, so hard his cock is leaking at the tip, and he finally looks like he's supposed to.

Like he'll ruin me all over again. I'm the one with a fist in his hair but he's the one with all the power. He could take himself away from me right now, and I believe what I said—if he doesn't fuck me, I'll die. Maybe I'll die anyway. That's the way the world works, isn't it? Sometimes you get kidnapped outside an airport.

Sometimes you get shot. Sometimes you do the shooting.

Every day you wake up and roll the dice.

His green eyes narrow. Something flashes through them, bright like gunfire, and he curses under his breath. I see the moment his self-control dissolves. It's the same moment his muscles bunch and he leans down to drag his teeth along my naked collarbone. It's a different kind of pain, sexy and glancing, and it makes me arch up toward him again.

This time Elijah doesn't deny me.

The cot is low, low enough for him to spread my legs with his big hands. He looks down between them to where I'm completely exposed. His eyes are a match, and I'm kindling. I'm ready to burn into a massive flame.

I need more.

Elijah takes himself in his fist and gives himself two absent strokes, jaw working. A flash of fear caresses the back of my neck. He really could hurt me.

He was honest about that.

A vicious fucking might actually damage me beyond repair.

But I'm already damaged beyond repair by him. I can't go back to the life I had before—not really. The last six months are proof. All those colorless days in my apartment and with my agent and doing all the mundane things from my mundane life tumble through my mind while I grit through this final wait. A lifetime of ordinary boredom when I could be doing *this*.

I can't take it, I can't take it—

The words are on my tongue when Elijah thrusts into me, all at once.

It's pure pain and pure pleasure, meeting each other like opposite storm fronts. He means to shield me from the worst of him like this, he tries his best, but it's not enough—this isn't enough. Not for him, and not for me. Three deep thrusts and he's crawling up over me, onto the cot, fucking so hard it takes the air from my lungs.

It hurts. It hurts bad enough that I moan in agony.

It's perfect.

Every time his hips meet mine there's an answering jolt of pain in the wound. The pain is nothing compared to how good it feels to be taken. Elijah's body is all tension and take. Mine is all give. This is how it's supposed to be, this, this, *this*.

Pleasure coils tight at the place he's using me now. He lets his head fall forward, his face in my neck. Lips on my skin. If he hadn't already stolen my breath with his body I'd lose it now. Every shallow tug on my lungs is supercharged with him. On fire with him.

I want him to burn me alive.

Being burned by him, being fucked and used and taken by him, is a thousand times better than lying here waiting for the pain to pass. Who does that?

Who just lays down and lets things happen to them?

Not me.

I didn't do it when I got kidnapped. I didn't do it when London found me. I don't know what I was thinking, trying to fit myself back into my old life when I'll never fit there again. The only place I fit is here, with Elijah, no matter how many times he tells me I won't.

His body tenses over mine and for a moment I think he's going to come, fast and hard, then leave me here, wanting, needing.

He lifts a hand. His fingers circle my throat. And a burst of energy knocks me back into my body. The painkillers tried to displace me but they failed. Like everything else, they failed. I lock my hands around his wrist and his eyes fly open, a low growl escaping him.

"Are you trying to stop me? You should try to stop me, goddamn it. Fight me off."

I'm on the forest floor again, tired and beaten and back in France. The ghosts of his hands on my wrists press into bone. "Say please."

His eyes widen, the green flaring bright. "You want me to beg you to stop me?"

He has to remember the way he said this to me that day in France. I know he does from the tick of his pulse in his jaw and the way his pupils blow out.

"Yes."

He kisses me hard, vicious, almost a bite. Still fucking. As animal as I've ever seen him. It came to this because of me. I wanted the beast, and I got him. "Stop me."

"That's not begging."

Elijah gives me three more hard thrusts and then we're moving. He's in control the way he is always in control. I hold my breath, bracing for tearing pain. It doesn't come. Somehow, he's maneuvered my injured self and his broken heart onto the cot so I'm on top.

I'm on top.

I splay my hands flat out on his chest.

It should be impossible, riding him like this, completely impossible. My core isn't strong enough. I'm dying, I'm dying. But I'm dying because it feels so good. Because Elijah hasn't let up. He's braced his hands on my hips, holding me up so the full pressure of my body isn't on the wound. It's all on him. On the thick length that's stretching me from the inside.

"Say please," I tell him again, even though I'm

the one close to begging, a shudder running up from my core all the way to the top of my head. I clench around him and he hisses.

"Stop me. Make me stop hurting you. Now."

"How am I supposed to stop you?"

"You have to." From this vantage point he's so handsome. He's still so powerful, even lying underneath me. It hasn't diminished his strength at all. "You have to. I'll be the death of you. I'll tear you apart. I'll hurt your wound. I'll fucking kill you."

I lean forward for more contact on my clit and get it. I'm swollen, oversensitive from wanting him and not having him. This new tug is an electric pressure that borders on sweet pain. "You're already the death of me. I'm not the same anymore. Ever since I met you, I'm not the same."

He lets go of my hips and lets me sink down onto him, his palms traveling up and up and up until his fingers are tangled in my hair. "Fuck, oh God, Holly, I—"

There's more he wants to say. The twist at the corner of his mouth makes it obvious. But I don't care. I can't care right now. He's at my limit and I work down against it anyway. He's at my limit and I still want more.

"All you have to do is beg me, Elijah, and I'll

make you stop."

"You're a liar."

"Yes." I am a liar. I never want him to stop, even if it hurts. Maybe I don't want him to stop *because* it hurts. My body was made in some strange way that wants pain.

I know I'm alive when it hurts.

"Damn it, Holly." He says my name through clenched teeth and it's almost like begging, though I know a man like Elijah North would never really beg. It would be beneath him. He would cajole and command and threaten but he won't beg.

Or will he?

I see his lips start to form the word, start to say please.

It's too late.

The winding, punishing orgasm that's been building and building shears off and explodes. And if I was trying to fight with him, if I was trying to take control—god, I don't know what I was doing. All of that is gone now. Destroyed. Elijah's body stills but mine doesn't. I'm aching and shuddering and clenching all over him.

His fingers tighten in my hair. They keep my face turned to his.

"Look at me."

The rough edge of his voice makes me peak again. It's nothing like *you need to rest*. It's nothing like the infinitely patient way he's been speaking to me, speaking around me, for the last thousand years. It's a voice that can't be disobeyed.

So I do look at him while I ride out the rest of this orgasm and its aftershocks. I trace the lightning in his eyes, the sunflower bursts of gold around his irises, and the dark shadow of guilt and pain and love behind all that new-leaf green.

He must sense the moment I come down because his fingers untangle themselves from my hair.

Elijah returns his big palms to my hips and holds.

I can't catch my breath and for a dizzying instant I think maybe he was right. Maybe I should have been resting instead of trying to fuck him like a crazy person.

But he's here, too. He's rocking his hips up to meet mine again. He's pushing himself up on one elbow so he can kiss me while he also braces me with his body.

I didn't know I could feel the wound until he does this, and then it's too late to feel anything but his release.

It takes him over. His thighs bunch underneath mine and he tips his head back, looking up toward salvation or just the ceiling. I graze my teeth over the line of his jaw and he turns into the touch. I'm still so hot for him, so wet I can hear it. Hear the low, soft grunts he makes as he comes. Hear the relief in his voice that he's worked so hard to hide from me.

When it's over he puts a hand to the back of my head and folds me into his shoulder, easing us both down to the cot. My skin hums. I could be in a field of bees, only I'm not, I'm in the basement of an abandoned church with one Elijah North taking up all the room on this narrow bed. Fine with me. Fine. His hard body feels like it's keeping the blood inside my skin. The bullet wound hurts, but it's a faraway pain, like it can't quite touch me.

Elijah reaches for the table next to the bed and something drops onto the floor with a plastic clatter. He doesn't move away from me to pick it up, only reaches for another bottle.

Those damned painkillers.

I'm too high from the sex to argue with him when he puts one on my tongue. I'm too high to do anything but sip water from the bottle he offers.

It kicks in fast. I have just enough time to sling an arm over his chest.

Stay, I mean to tell him. There are other things I want to tell him, too, so much I have to say.

Too late.

Sleep closes in.

CHAPTER EIGHT

ADAM

L ONDON'S APARTMENT RAISES more questions than it answers.

Questions are easy to come by, here on the couch, listening to the unsteady rumble of traffic out on the street.

Most people's apartments—or houses or dungeons—give away lots of information about them. People tell their whole life story in what they keep and what they throw away. But I find I have a particular interest in my surroundings. This is because of my particular interest in London Frank. *Particular interest* is an understatement of the kind that makes me laugh out loud, even when I'm alone in a silent apartment.

And I am alone in a silent apartment. Her silent apartment.

It's been days. Long enough for London to go running to her authority of choice and tell them that I, Adam Bisset, have taken up residence on the hand-me-down couch in her one-bedroom apartment. It's an option that's open to her. Then again, it would implicate her, too.

And London Frank can't afford to be implicated.

If I were a good man, I would disappear right now, before she returns from her shopping. I would disappear and I would lose myself on the opposite side of the planet.

Naturally, disappearing comes with its own set of risks. If I disappear, there will be no one here when they come for her. Someone will always come for London Frank.

How could they not?

I couldn't help myself. I knew damn well that I shouldn't come here, and yet I did.

And there is the thing I can hardly admit even in the privacy of my own thoughts.

I don't want to disappear.

I've spent a lifetime in the shadowy spaces between where real people eat and fuck and get married. London lives in the light. If it were possible to be there with her…

London has been gone fifteen minutes when I tire of lying on the couch, staring up at the old plastered ceiling. The bullet that tried for my life didn't hit anything too important, and I took it out before any major infection set in. It would have been more dramatic to die. Ah, well. Now I have the opportunity to go through her things.

The main room is a kitchen and living room in one. It's not terrible, for New York City real estate—close but not cramped. The appliances are old but scrubbed clean.

Either she cares a lot about kitchen maintenance or she barely eats here.

The refrigerator speaks to the latter. London has three bottles of strawberry-infused water, half a bag of baby carrots, and a takeout container of unknown origin.

She came home the other night smelling like a coffee shop, so she must eat there—or somewhere else. I can picture her a hundred places in the city, feet wrapped around the rungs of a barstool, neon lights in her hair.

I can't picture her standing over the stove, stirring a pot of noodles. She does have noodles, two boxes in a slim cupboard above the fridge.

Oh—traveling. She would have been traveling before for her work as an influencer.

But she's not traveling now. How could she, really? Posting her face all over a public profile would bring the NSA running faster than she could count to ten.

So could my presence here.

It's a toss-up.

The living room doesn't offer much in the way of new things to look at. There's the couch and the crocheted blanket I've been sleeping under. A television on an IKEA stand, with a fake potted plant perched nearby. I've been in here for days. I know every leaf on that plant.

I pass by the bathroom in the narrow hall separating Holly's bedroom from the rest of the space. Her medicine cabinet is practically bare. A bottle of Tylenol—that's it. No prescriptions. I searched the medicine cabinet the last time she went shopping, hoping for something stronger.

Nothing.

The one place I haven't been is London's bedroom.

The door's open when I get there. Open wide. It's almost flat against the inner wall, so I can lean against the doorframe and look in. I've assessed hundreds of rooms over the course of my career. None of them have made my hair stand on end. Not like this.

At first glance there's nothing out of the ordinary. A full-size mattress with a rumpled white comforter sits close to one wall, with just enough room on the side for a person of London's size to squeeze past. A slim end table holds up a nondescript lamp. The closet space isn't anything to write home about—a long closet set into one wall. Shallow. So shallow it can't hold all of London's clothes, which are stacked on the floor, bursting at the seams. This is the first hint of her former influencer life.

She has a wardrobe.

But it doesn't look like it's recently been in use. The hamper wedged into a corner of the closet only has a few items at the bottom. She hasn't been changing in and out of various looks for photoshoots. I would be shocked to discover she's been sneaking out to take photos. It wouldn't be much of a travel shoot for London.

So there are the clothes.

And then there is the shelf.

It's one shelf, also IKEA-chic, snugged up in a space below the narrow window at the front of the room. The window looks down over a New York City street as nondescript as anywhere else. That doesn't mean it's safe. That doesn't mean they won't find us. But that's old information. What interests me is the contents of the shelf.

The top two squares are filled with records.

Records leaning against each other in a tilted slope toward the left side. On top of the shelf, in a place of prominence, is a blush pink record player. This, at least, looks perfect for an Instagram shoot. Something sent to her by a company that wanted her influence, no doubt. Women like London get this kind of thing all the time. That's why they go into careers on social media, or at least side jobs there.

I would expect London's apartment to be full of these kinds of gifts, or bribes, or payments.

It's not.

Aside from her clothes, the record player is the only obvious sign of her career. And maybe I'm wrong. Maybe she bought this for herself to go with her record collection.

I didn't intend to come into the room when I stood up. Only to look. To canvas. The records change my plans. My fingers itch to separate them from each other and read the titles. It's the same aching itch I have to touch London whenever she's in the same room, which is nearly always.

A deep breath to steady myself turns into an exercise in restraint. I can smell her. The light floral soapy scent of her shampoo is all over the blanket, and she's left it tumbled and open, like she just climbed out of it. The bed is a trap. It's the records that hook me at the center of my chest and tug me across the threshold.

The fact that I hesitated has made all of this more illicit and more irresistible. If I'd just walked in like I own both the bedroom *and* London Frank, I wouldn't get to feel this blend of shame and exhilaration.

My feet meet the rug and it gives. The rug, like everything else, is shockingly secondhand. It's endearing as hell to know that a person like London, beautiful, well-traveled London, furnishes her apartment with comfortable castoffs. I fight off the urge to sink down to my knees and run my palms over the fabric ridges.

The rug ends where the shelf begins.

This is more intimate than rifling through her underwear drawer. Make no mistake—I want to do that, too. So much that if she ever knew, she'd call me a sick bastard and change the locks. I want to look at the records more. Is it an obsession if it makes you want to go through a person's records more than you want to see their lingerie?

Perhaps.

I test the paperboard sleeves of the records and my heart races like I've hooked a finger into the waistband of her panties. It hurts to stand, as cavalier as I'm being about it.

What hurts more is the absence of her in this apartment. I'm six inches from the side of her bed and it's a joke. A furniture taunt. I could have her in that bed. What I wouldn't give to have her in that bed, to have my fingertips on her skin instead of on these records—

I pull one out at random, take off the sleeve, and drop it onto the record player. My grandpa had one of these when he was alive. An Army man. He would have been ashamed of what his son had become. He would have been ashamed of me, too. I suppose it's just as well he died of a heart attack decades ago.

The needle drops into the groove and the soulful voice of Etta James fills the space.

Maybe she's listened to this, too, standing in this very spot. Maybe she was only dressed in panties and a bra. Maybe she was wearing nothing. Her body would have been relaxed. It wouldn't be like it is with me. London pretends to be at ease but I know she's not. She knows what I'm capable of.

"What are you doing?"

London's voice is a spear through *At Last*. My hand goes to the bullet wound before I can stop myself, skin tightening. I've been swaying a little with the music. Mistake.

She's planted her feet in the doorway, eyes dark with suspicion. London has both arms around a paper grocery bag and her lips in a thin line.

I can't stand it. Can't stand the frown, can't stand the tense set to her shoulders, can't stand any of it. It's only a few steps across the room.

When I reach for the bag she turns slightly away, eyes narrowing. "What are you—"

"Don't fight with me. Don't argue." London releases her death grip on the groceries and lets me put them on the bed. And then I reach for her hand. "Dance with me."

She has already taken my hand by the time the words are past my lips. Already stepped toward me, still in her winter jacket. Oh, London. You can't resist me, either.

It could be the music, but I suspect it's something else that makes her move in closer. Long eyelashes flutter closed over eyes like the forest at night. She sighs. It sounds like surrender. "What are you doing?" This time, it's more of a plea than an accusation.

"Dancing with you."

I lift my arm and London twirls underneath it. The breath goes out of my lungs. A man who has been shot should keep his arms below his shoulders to avoid worsening the wound. I've worsened it. And I've had a vision of her in a white dress, with flowers in her hair.

She finishes the turn and searches my face. "You look like shit."

"You only keep Tylenol in your apartment."

"You looking for something harder?"

"Why? You got a stash of pot in here somewhere? It's not even illegal here."

"Sorry. Only Tylenol. I might be able to spring for Advil, if you play your cards right, but no promises. I might give you essential oils instead."

I search her beautiful hazel eyes. Sometimes people are careful about what drugs they keep around because they dealt with addiction. "Did you use?"

"Cocaine," she says, her voice flat and matter of fact.

"I'm sorry."

"Don't be. I'm cleaned up. It doesn't control me anymore."

My voice comes out soft. "I'm glad."

"Should you even be dancing right now? You just got shot."

So it hurts. So does everything. "There's nowhere else I'd rather be."

"That's a slick line. I don't fall for guys with slick lines. Not anymore."

"But you used to?"

"Used to do a lot of things. Used to be an influencer. A couple million people like to watch me splash around on the beach at Bali or walk barefoot in the desert in Egypt."

"Nice work if you can get it."

She gives a delicate snort laugh. "Yeah, what they didn't see was the hours it took to do my hair so it would have those beachy waves before my toes even touched the water. Or the sunburn I got from posing for two hours to get the perfect shot."

"And you met a lot of slick guys this way, huh?"

"It's the party scene. I started off wanting to travel the world. Wanderlust. My parents had it, too. I never wanted to stay in one place. The Instagram, the photos. It was all for fun at first. Then I started getting contracts as an influencer. All you have to do is say you drank this coconut water or wear those clothes. I thought, what's the harm? I started getting invited to all these parties. Meeting models and celebrities. Doing drugs."

"And you're done with that now."

"Definitely done with the drugs. Maybe done with the whole scene. Instagram. TikTok. Selfies. Makeup. Traveling the world. It's a lot scarier when you've been on the run across the Italian countryside. You realize just how dangerous that world can be."

I sweep her in a circle around her old embroidered armchair. It makes my side ache, but I don't really fucking care, not when her hair's flowing around her shoulders. "You don't have to swear off traveling. Or selfies. It could happen without the drugs."

She shrugs. "I don't know. It's not like it was important work, anyway. Convincing people they should drink coconut water or making them feel envious of my life."

"Not important?"

"Not like Holly. She's a bestselling author. Millions of people read her words."

"And millions of people see your photos."

She scrunches her nose, looking adorable. "It's not the same."

"No," I say slowly. "Not the same, but still important. You give people a sense of adventure, even when they're afraid to take that step for themselves."

"Don't make me sound all noble and interesting. I don't even like coconut water."

That makes me laugh, which hurts more than the dancing. I press my lips to the top of her head. God, she smells good. Not like coconut, though. Sweeter than that. "Maybe not noble, but you're definitely interesting, London Frank. Don't let anyone tell you otherwise."

CHAPTER NINE

ELIJAH

HOLLY SLEEPS LIKE we're in a five-star hotel, all pink and flushed beneath the sheet on the cot.

I stayed until my leg fell asleep from hanging off the side. If there's one thing I can't afford, it's to be caught with pins and needles in one of my feet. The city breathes around us. With every inhale our enemies get closer. This is a hunting expedition, and we're the prey.

I find a blanket and tuck Holly in, then take the chair by her side to keep watch.

There's nothing to see except the way the blankets rise and fall with every even breath she takes. The rhythm is enough to hypnotize a man, and it does. I become attuned to the steady in and out, in and out, in and out. I watch, enraptured, while my mind works through the decisions that need to be made. Though they're already made, really. Everything has already been chosen for us.

It was chosen years ago, and it's time to tell Holly the truth.

As soon as she wakes up.

She sleeps for a long time, alive and breathing. So long that my own eyelids grow heavy. At some point toward dawn I close my eyes for a moment. Soldiers learn how to sleep in short, necessary bursts. I open my eyes when I hear Holly shifting on the cot.

It's heartbreaking, watching her wake up.

She stretches her arms over her head. I reach to stop her—too late. Holly stops herself with a wince. A gasp. I shouldn't have fucked her last night. It was wrong.

It was wrong, but the memory of it has me hard right now.

Holly turns her head, her sleepy gaze finding my face. "Don't regret it."

She means the sex. That's the only part of this I don't regret.

Most of all I regret what happens next.

Every part of me resists telling her. My calves tense. My heart slows. I'd rather walk to the ends of the earth. There's no other choice. "We're in danger."

Holly rubs at her eyes with one hand. "I know."

"You don't." I run a hand over my face. I want to throw my body in front of the bullet for her, but I already failed. "It's not a matter of if they'll find us, it's when. You have to know what to do when they arrive. Because it's not about murder, not really."

"Elijah—"

"It's about treason. Casus belli. It's an act of war."

She looks stricken, and I hate myself right now. "I'm sorry."

"Don't be sorry. You were defending yourself. And me. I'm not angry, but I have to... I have to tell you this. I have to prepare you for what happens next."

A hard swallow. "Which is?"

"They will spin it like it's an act against country. His crimes won't matter. And—" I swallow against the knot in my throat. A million times I've been in the hands of the enemy. There's always been a little bit of relief. A little hope that the pain will end. Even death means a cease to the suffering. The thought of Holly in the enemy's hands is a new type of fear. It freezes me solid, ice from the inside out. "The military doesn't need to follow the rules. They don't need an arrest warrant, they don't need to give you a lawyer. Not for an enemy combatant. You can disappear, if that's what they want."

"Okay." Her voice only shakes a little. "So we need to get out of the country."

Yes and no. Being out of the country would only delay the inevitable. And there's no way she can be moved right now without risking her life. I refuse to do that. I know it's damned hypocritical because I was willing to fuck her raw, but I only have so much control where she's concerned. "When we're caught, you need to say that I pulled the trigger."

I can tell how much it hurts her to sit up with such speed and force, but Holly does it anyway. "I'm not going to do that. I'm the one who shot him, and I won't—" She winces, and I reach for the bottle of painkillers. "You are not going to drug me out of this conversation."

"I'm not going to let anything happen to you." I pull my hand back from the painkillers and stand up. She has to lay down. Has to rest, before the storm breaks over us. "That's asking too much. You protected me by shooting him. Now it's my turn to protect you."

She gets her feet over the side of the cot before I can stop her.

"Holly, what the hell—" I try to stop her, but

she's throwing all her weight against me. It would tear her wound apart if I insist, so I'm forced to hover around her, ready to catch her if she falls. "I swear to god I will tie you to this bed with no remorse."

"Good," she says. "At least that would be the real you."

There's nowhere to go except back, and she's pushing herself into me, butting against me, with such a furious insistence that I could laugh if we weren't waiting for the end of the world.

Holly puts both hands up on my chest and pushes.

My hands come up on instinct. She can't be doing this, can't be using her body like this, not when it's injured. And she knows it.

She lets herself go, a wicked streak in her eyes, and I land in the chair with her between my legs. Holly clambers up onto my lap, her breath hitching.

The sheet falls.

All my noble intentions fall with it.

Because she's straddling my lap, reaching down for the fly of my pants. And I'm running my hands over the curves of her hips and down to pinch her ass. Hard.

I want to leave bruises. Even if they come for

us, she'll have my fingerprints on her skin. Fucked up? Yes. But I never claimed to be otherwise.

Even through my jeans I can feel her pussy, warm and wet against my cock. It would be so easy to slide inside, to pump inside her toward oblivion. It's the only heaven I'll ever know. The only heaven I'll ever need. I pull her flush against my erection, and she whimpers. The pressure feels incredible for me, but I know it's too much for her. The taut denim is too rough against her secret flesh. I drop my head back and stare at the cold, dark ceiling, reveling in the uneven pleasure. Above us is a place of worship. What kind of god would make men hard and rough? Women are so soft, like flower petals. I'll grind her into pieces on the altar of my lust.

I stroke myself with her sex, rubbing her against me, enveloping my cock, lifting her entire body with every thrust. I'm not even inside her yet, and I'm about to come. Only that makes me stop. I sit back, breathing hard, trying to get myself under control.

Holly's hands move quickly on my zipper. All these hours I've spent wrestling her into that damn cot and it's still come to this—gripping her flesh, lifting my hips so my cock is freed from layers of cloth. My cock stands proud and thick between us, already glistening with pre cum.

I touch the tip to wet my finger and push it into her mouth. One finger. Two. Her eyes go wide, but she doesn't fight me. She accepts me as I fuck her mouth this way, two fingers that taste like my come, rubbing my forefinger over her tongue, reveling in the damp heat. "That's right," I say, my voice low. "Show me how bad you want my come."

And bless her, she does. She forms a beautiful suction on my fingers, and my cock flexes in the cool air between us. I push farther back, touching the back of her throat, and she gags around my hand. Even that makes me harder, the sound and the convulsion a reward all its own.

"Go ahead and fuck me, sweetheart. Work me good."

She's determined and already lifting her hips. Effort shines in her face while she works herself down onto me. It has to be painful. My job here is to stop her, to convince her to heal. The entry wound has healed better than the exit. Her insides are still torn to shit.

Then her wet heat envelopes me, and her inner muscles clench my cock, and I forget that I existed outside this moment. There's only bliss and endless pleasure.

"Hold still," I say between clenched teeth. I grasp her hips and thrust from beneath her, forcing my cock inside her, again and again, holding her suspended above me. It's only slightly better than letting her fuck me. She still has to clench her muscles while I use her body. She could start bleeding from what I'm doing. But she submits so sweetly, almost as if she knows how badly I've needed this, how hard I've had to hold myself back from her. Even as I changed the dressing on her wound and pulled the blanket up to her neck, I've imagined taking out my cock. I've imagined fucking my fist until white liquid covers her face.

My brothers were right to turn their backs on me. Liam was right when he questioned my treatment of Holly. Look what I'm doing to her—and she's so fucking beautiful, color spread across her cheeks and her neck, tits bouncing beneath the sports bra.

As quickly as I started, I stop. I lift her up from my lap so she's an inch above the tip of my cock. It hurts, the dry air on my private flesh. It hurts to be outside of her.

"No," she moans, her hips rocking uselessly where my cock used to be.

"Promise me," I say, licking my lips. "I'll only

let you come if you promise."

"Promise what?"

"Promise you'll say I shot him."

Her eyes are lust-dazed and dark. They go wide when I say that. It takes her slow seconds to focus on me. Outrage and desire mix in her brown gaze. "What?"

"You heard me."

"Don't… No. You can't be serious."

"Stone cold," I say, resting her ass on my thighs. That gives me space to bring my hands to her front, to run my thumb through her wet folds. God, she feels good. I want her around my cock again, but not without this. "You want this cock, you promise me."

Fire flares in her dark eyes. "You're sure I'll give in."

My thumb finds her clit, and I circle, circle, circle. She gasps and wriggles in my arms. There is no country safe enough. There is no safehouse hidden enough. We will be found. The only way to save her is this. "Promise me, and I'll fuck you until you cry."

Her thighs tremble around me. Her hips give a small, telling jolt. "No. Please."

"It's so easy," I coax, an asshole to the last. "So easy to give me what I want. Then I'll make you feel good. I'll fill you up and come inside you."

She shudders. Her eyes drift closed. "Please."

I stroke her with blunt, harsh movements. I'm not trying to make her rise gently. I want her spilling over and desperate. She has a strong will, but I have time on my side. Seconds turn into minutes. They might even become hours as I fuck her with my fingers, keeping her on the edge, never letting her fall into orgasm. Tears fall down her cheeks, squeezed from beneath tightly closed eyelids. "Promise me, sweetheart. That's all you have to do."

She should have known I'd get my way, whether I used the pain medicine to distract or sex to fuck her into oblivion. She's rocking on my legs, arousal dripping onto my jeans, lips parted in a sexy pant, whole body moving in time with my thumb. I'm relentless, bringing her inexorably to the pinnacle only to hold her there. She can't move. Can't go anywhere, can only take it. The tears come faster now, they flood down her cheeks, because she knows she's lost.

The words are a broken whisper. "I promise."

Relief sweeps through me, wiping out all thought. I slam her down onto my cock, and she comes immediately, her muscles clenching and quivering around me, liquid desire sliding down my cock to my balls, and I come in a hard, endless pulse that coats her inside with come.

CHAPTER TEN

HOLLY

Washing up at a utility sink shouldn't be sexy, but it is.

I shouldn't spend my time memorizing the dips and lines of Elijah's hard body, but I do.

He rubs soap between his big palms. Water runs over his knuckles in white suds. Such mundane movements but the sex has given them a surreal, shimmering quality. A joke about being in a movie comes to mind and flits back out again. He looks too serious for jokes. So serious. So tense. Like someone might burst into this dark church at any moment.

I see the shadow of fear in his eyes when he looks into the mirror above the sink, but he blinks it away in an instant. Did I imagine it? Does he truly believe that the net is closing in around us, or is it just his nature to be prepared? God knows he's earned the right. Survival has been the focus of his entire life, and not in the abstract way it is for other people. We're all trying to make it in the world. Elijah carves out heartbeat after heartbeat.

It's my new mission to convince him this isn't true.

"Elijah," I say, and his green eyes meet mine in the blackened mirror. They're so intense that I'm winded. What was I going to say to him, anyway? That he's wrong about the world around us? That soon, we'll be able to sneak out into the dark and disappear? I didn't have a plan when I shot that gun and I don't have a plan now. I just have a fierce, delirious need to prove to him that we'll survive. We can survive anything as long as we're together.

"I love you." The words fall out of my mouth like stones to the bottom of the ocean, swift and sure of their way down. It isn't a solution. It won't protect us from bullets, but it doesn't have to. It has a power all its own, and the love builds inside me until I'm bursting.

He whirls to face me, stunned for a single, breathless moment.

Three things happen at once in the pause before he speaks.

There's a sound of wood splintering on stone. Elijah blinks, and when his eyes open again, something flashes through them, onyx through emerald. It looks like heartbreak but it's gone too soon to pin it down. And he moves.

"What are you doing?" It's a pointless question, wasted breath, because as soon as he's between me and the bathroom door it's obvious.

It's so horribly, awfully obvious.

He was right.

I'm out of time to prove to him that we'll be okay in the end.

We will not be all right. Love doesn't conquer all.

Men swarm down into the basement, too many to count, a swarm of black shields and weaponry. They're multiplying, shouting. My question is swallowed up in the storm of noise. Something loud explodes in the next room, toward the cell, but nothing heats or burns. A flashbang? I discover I've put my hands over my ears and I'm too late.

My entire skull rings with the noise.

Elijah's shadow falls away from me.

He's falling, too. There are so many people, too many people, and they're coordinated. They knock him down and he gets back up. The bathroom is too small to fight in, far too small. The rim of the sink presses coldly into my back. I'm afraid to let go of my ears in case my brain spills out, but I do, I do, because I have to reach for him.

I get a fist into his t-shirt.

It's ripped away.

A frustrated scream I can't hear scorches my throat, fear corroding the raw flesh. They're kicking him. Killing him. How is ever going to survive this? He won't, not unless—

I lurch forward and throw my body down over his. There's a chance if I can hold on.

There's a chance.

I can't hold on.

How many people have crowded into the bathroom? Six? Ten? Four hands dig into my skin. I don't know what I'm shouting as they drag me away. I get one arm hooked through his. It comes to nothing. My nails rake across his bicep, leaving red trails behind.

He's hidden from me by the black outfits and combat gear and I feel something like vertigo. Something like the disembodied horror of losing a tooth. They're dragging me, carrying me, toward the stairs.

I'm not going to get back to him. If they take me out of here and I die, I won't be able to get back to him.

I let myself go limp, the full weight of me

pulling down toward the floor. My heel catches on the stairs and it sends a bolt of pain up through my leg. At least I have contact with the bottom step and I dig it in.

Sounds filter through the ringing in my ears. One of the men, cursing me out steadily and fluently. Knuckles meeting someone's cheekbone. The grunt as a punch clears the air from someone's lungs.

And a high, keening cry.

Me.

I'm the one making that noise, and it strangles itself into words. They're having to work for this. A detached part of me is proud that I'm putting up a fight, even though it hurts like a motherfucker. There's no way I haven't undone all Elijah's careful healing. Even that doesn't hurt as much as being separated from him.

He's still fighting, but they're piling on now with me out of the way. "Leave him alone," I shout, a hot tear dripping into my mouth.

Leaving Elijah alone is not on the agenda for the day and anger screws itself into my spine. They're monsters. They're monstrous. There are too many hands and arms to keep track of. One of those hands rises and comes down to meet the side of Elijah's head and I scream again. A black-clad arm locks itself around my neck and pulls. I claw at body armor and get no response.

He drags me up two more stairs, his partner huffing beside him. It's a narrow space and I kick out again and again, trying to sink my heels into their shins, into the steps, anything. Anywhere.

Elijah falls again and the metallic anger is replaced with fear the color of his blood. It's red like paint, red like pretend, but it's real enough to stop my heart.

We're almost to the top of the stairs now and an animal cry tears itself out of me. I don't want to lose sight of Elijah. I want to keep my eyes on him for as long as possible. In the process I manage to wedge myself against the wall, one man's hand pinned underneath my shoulder.

For a moment we're face to face.

I can hardly make out his features through the haze of my tears. He's half hidden under a tactical helmet, dark glasses covering his eyes, and if I could rip those glasses off I would. Letting go of his arm to do it isn't an option.

My only option left is to beg.

It cracks me open, having to do this, but what wouldn't I do for Elijah?

Nothing. The answer is nothing.

"Please," I sob at my blurred reflection in his

glasses, then swallow the crying like it's broken glass. I set my teeth. "Please don't do this. You're killing him. Your friends are killing him. You could make them stop."

His arm tenses under my hand and then he moves, too fast for me to fight him off. His fingers lock tight around my biceps. I'm caught in a trap now, a trap of my own making, goddamn it. This man's options are practically unlimited. He could lift me straight upward, he could throw me over his shoulder, he could throw me back against the wall hard enough to knock me out.

I freeze in place. "Let me stay with him. Please, please, let me stay with him."

The corner of his mouth turns down and that single, tiny movement makes my whole body thrill with hope. There—a crack in the armor. Please, please, let it be enough to let me reach the man beneath the hard asshole facade. I can see him. He's so close. This man must be someone's husband. He must be someone's father. Some-one's son. He must still be those things even while he's leaving bruises on my arms.

"Please. I can't let him die."

His mouth returns to its stoic line. Hope snuffs itself out in my heart, weak as a candle in rain. A sob balls itself up at the back of my throat.

He's gone. The moment is gone. In the bathroom, a fist connects with Elijah's face and his head snaps back. I see it out of the corner of my eye but it might as well be playing on my own personal movie screen.

The man who has my life in his hands gives me a sharp tug. Elijah disappears behind the black shirts. He's gone, he's gone, and as much as I twist, as much as I fight, as much as I hurt myself, I can't get him back in sight.

"Forget you ever knew him." The voice in my ear is as rough as the sound of his boots on the ground. It's the sound of the end of the world. "That's the best advice I can give you. No matter what happens next, he's already dead."

CHAPTER ELEVEN

ELIJAH

THE INTERROGATION ROOM where I'm going to die is the least impressive place I've ever seen.

They've taken it straight out of a B-movie set with its drain in the floor and its cinder block walls and ungodly fluorescent lights. No, of course that's not true. The movies stole from this room. What's that saying about art imitating life?

I'm doing a pretty good imitation of dying. This room is doing a pretty good imitation of a morgue. And these guys could be doing an autopsy of all my life's mistakes. They could be. They're busy, though.

Three guys in a room, me tied to a chair, and oh—here comes another one.

Another fist, I mean.

It connects with the soft part of my gut and I'm past the point where I can stop making noise. That's one thing the movies never get right.

Those guys are always crying too early or too late. I'm not going to cry, but I will grunt and cough.

It's not some tough guy routine. It's just that I used all my tears up early in life. Look at me, getting all poetic in my last moments. The thing no one ever tells you is that a man can be aware of his own death for a cruel amount of time before it happens.

My resistance to the process isn't speeding things along, either.

Or maybe it is.

The bastard with the blue t-shirt leans into my face. It's not standard Army issue, that blue T-shirt, but then nothing about this is officially sanctioned. This is all dark ops, secret room shit that the higher ups would rather pretend didn't happen. "Tell us what she knows."

"Go fuck yourself."

He punches me for the pleasure of it. One of my teeth is loose, maybe more, and I don't have much time before my jaw gets broken. I taste salt and blood.

When Blue Shirt gets close I spit it into his face.

He breaks a rib in return.

There's a dance to torture. A rhythm.

The rhythm of *this* torture, it's fast. You get

more information if you draw it out, the same way I drew out playing with Holly's clit while she rocked on my lap. But this guy doesn't seem to know the finer points of torture. Or he doesn't care.

That means I'll wind up dead sooner rather than later. Small favors.

It takes me a minute to cough the pain and the blood out before I hang limp. I'm tied up with both hands behind my back, wrists wrapped together behind the chair, chest exposed for the beating. I wasn't wearing a shirt when they grabbed me and I'm not wearing one now.

It's not an amazing way to go, but it's about the death I expected.

I always had this coming, from the moment my dad threw me down a well and went to bed to sleep it off. Sometimes he'd come back to see if I survived the night. Sometimes he wouldn't remember for days. You had to be strong to survive the well, but you knew, you always knew, that it would end in terrible agony.

That's for guys like me. Not for the Hollys of the world. Only good things for her. A man who stays faithful. Probably a doctor who coaches their kid's softball team. A long life. And at the end, a peaceful drifting away during sleep.

"Your girl, your pretty little girl, her skin all smooth and white. It's a beautiful canvas. They're holding her for me." The man gives me a small, almost abashed smile, as if he's a boy proud of a frog he's brought home to his mother. It's so disturbing it sends a shiver skating over my skin. "That's one of the benefits of being senior here. You get to keep the good parts to yourself. And she's a very, very good part. I commend you on your choice."

"Don't you fucking touch her."

He grins.

My blood goes cold and still, stuttering in my veins, but I don't let the sharp fear show on my face. I can't show them fear. I can't show them how badly I've fucked up.

This situation is why I never got close to anyone. This is why I walked away from everyone who ever walked into my life. It's why I've separated myself from my brothers for all these years. It's why I fought so hard not to fall for Holly.

You can't fight the demons I fight when you have something to lose.

And finally, with Holly, I have everything to lose.

Everything.

I tried to warn her that this would happen. That the clock on our time together would wind down into the most horrific scenario I can imagine. Not the torture per se. I've been on the receiving end of enough of it to know that this isn't the real hardship. The real hardship is being separated from her while it happens. Not that I want her to see this. As long as she doesn't see, she won't have to remember.

My mind wanders to wherever she is. In my head no one ever put their hands on her. She's still safe and untouched. That's a fantasy. I'll allow myself the one while I wait. One turns into another. It doesn't take long. Her eyes on me. Her hands on me. Her body stretched out against mine, warm and sleepy.

At some point I stop imagining the way things were and start picturing the way things could have been if everything else in my life had gone another way.

But if I had been normal, if I had a family that gave a shit, I might never have met her in the first place. I'd do all of this again if it meant being with her.

They take a minute to gather themselves, my team of assigned torturers. Blood from a cut on my forehead stings my eyes while they circle around me. I don't bother looking. Their shadows will get closer, and when they do, more damage will come. I flex my hands behind the chair and try to keep circulation moving through them. Pointless tasks to pass the time.

A fist into my gut yanks me back to the present.

"Of course if you tell me everything I want you know," he continues conversationally, as if he didn't just strike a fatal blow, as if he isn't panting and sweating from exertion, "then I won't have any reason to question her. She'd be safe."

This is a lie, of course. It's part of the torture dance. The rhythm.

Two of them come close and tip the chair. My skull helpfully breaks the fall. Blurred-out vision is a good sign that they'll crack it soon enough and then I'll be out of my misery. One well-placed kick to the head and it's lights out.

My heart speeds up at the thought. When I die here, that's the end. There's no hope for Holly. I'm the reason she's valuable to them at all. If I'm no longer on this plane of existence they'll kill her and bag her and the world will never know where she went.

The only way to help her is to stay alive.

The only thing to look at down here on the

floor is boots.

Black boots.

Steel-toed boots.

The boots move out of sight and my body braces. It's hard to fathom the exact pain of getting kicked with steel-toed boots. My muscles know it's coming anyway.

They wait until I relax, then aim the first kick at my gut.

Something comes loose in there. Bone, maybe. Part of an organ. Probably something essential, but it's sheared away now and my entire gut feels thick with blood. This is the perfect interval to land another kick, and—

Fuck.

They do.

One of them puts a boot on my knee and presses down. He starts slow and increases the pressure until the full weight of him is on the joint. I'd be a surgery case if I could get out of here. Gather round, med students. See what a broken body really is. But that's the joke, isn't it? I'm not getting out.

The pressure releases from my knee at the same moment another kick lands in my stomach. I taste pennies and spit blood in the general direction of the closest steel-toed boots.

"Tell me who's paying you. Who hired you to kill the colonel."

"No one," I grind out.

"If you don't tell me, I'll have to ask the pretty girl with the brown eyes and the brown hair and the pretty tits. You ever fuck those tits? Bet they feel great around your dick."

"I'm going to beat your face in with my fist," I say between gritted teeth.

"That's my line, dickwad."

My torturers hold a brief meeting somewhere above my head and decide to pick me up off the floor. This is not an improvement. I thought they'd kick me to death down here, which I had planned for, and now what? Now the chair's back up in its place.

One of them stands in front of me, the toe of his boot on top of my foot, and deals glancing blows to my face while another one unties my hands.

My shoulders scream from being held in this position and suddenly freed, the pain a warning that it's a trap. And of course it is. Of course my hands are only free for a minute, and then they're above my head, held in place by a thick length of rope. Turns out there's rope hanging from the ceiling. Every good torture factory needs rope hanging down from the ceiling.

Enough rope to hold a man in place for a series of electric shocks.

Water is the first part of the plan. At first I think there's two of them coming with the bucket but it's only double vision. It's the ringleader, Blue Shirt, his face split open with a smile.

"You're going to talk," he says, his grin gruesome and deranged.

"The prisoner's dilemma is a paradox," I tell him.

He pauses, glares at me, then dumps the bucket over my head. It's hell frozen solid and it stings the cuts on my skin and forces a gasp out of me. Not my best moment. "What the fuck did you say?"

"You wanted to talk, I'll talk. The prisoner's dilemma. It's a paradox." Goosebumps pinch the back of my neck and sprint down my arms. My stomach is hot with the injuries and cold with the water and I'll give them some credit. It's miserable. "It's where two people in two different rooms are questioned. That's what happening here, in case you needed me to spell it out."

In exchange for this I get a punch to the jaw that snaps my head around, followed by the first electric shock. He aims it at exposed skin above my collarbone and it arcs around the front of my throat and squeezes. Pain follows a second later.

My teeth grind together. It's a hell of a thing when your teeth fight to crush themselves. The pressure in my jaw from the combined reflex to shiver and the activated muscles keeping my teeth shut tight could make my head fall off and flop onto the floor. They'd be so pissed if that happened. A headless guy can't say a damn thing against the woman he loves.

I think of Holly in that basement in France.

I heard her voice before I saw her. I was hurt then, too.

Were you shot?

In the back. It's all very Roman.

She'd touched me then, her touch lighter than air. Holly had no idea who I was. She had no idea what I'd already done to her. No idea what I would do. Her fingertips circled the wound. I heard the hitch in her breath. And what did she say?

You can't die.

I'm serious.

So serious, and all for a small wound. If Holly saw me now she wouldn't know where to put her hands. There are too many cuts and bruises. Too much blood. A smile twists the corners of my mouth and Blue Shirt notices. He doesn't like it. He stomps one foot down on mine, and damn it, I don't have my own pair of steel-toed boots. At least one toe breaks. Maybe more.

"So Prisoner A—that's me in this example, fuckface." Grinding pain splinters off from my foot and drives into my chin. "Prisoner A betrays Prisoner B in order to earn himself a better deal."

"Go ahead," he says, laughing his demonic laugh. "You aren't getting a good deal, though."

"Yes, well, that's a flaw in your plan. You're not incentivizing me to speak." The word *incentivizing* comes out jumbled. I've taken quite a few punches to the mouth. "You're only punishing me for not speaking. It's only half as effective."

In light of my explanation the three of them decide to work as a team. One of them pulls my head back, exposing my throat. The second one lines up a boot with my other foot. And Blue Shirt goes for the heart.

The electricity is a nice touch, it really is. It lights up every muscle in a sick parody of the way I feel when I'm with Holly. With my head back like this it's impossible to move through it. *You can't die*, whispers Holly from somewhere else. Oh, sweetheart, but I can.

When it's over my stomach is twisted inside out. Blue Shirt tops it off with a blow across the face. A tooth comes loose. I cough it out before I can choke on it. "Prisoner B, though. She has the same idea. She betrays A so she can get a better deal."

"Your girl's going to sell herself to get free, is that right? And leave you hanging here by your wrists while we fuckin' electrocute you? Yeah. Yeah, I could see that happening."

Someone has their fingers in my hair and there's no way for me to leverage myself back to the ground. I am suspended on the back two legs of the chair. My neck could snap at any moment.

"And that's how—" My own cough interrupts me. It's soaked in blood, soaked in salt and metal, and it's the taste of something gone very wrong. It's the taste of imminent death. It would be dramatic to even think it if it weren't so true. "That's how they both end up with the worst possible outcome. That's how they both end up being tortured by the dark side of the Army until they fucking die. You want to talk? Let's talk about that."

CHAPTER TWELVE

HOLLY

THE MAN IN the room with me folds his arms over his barrel chest and taps his fingers over his elbow. He does this every time he stops to consider me, which is often.

My head aches from crying, from screaming, from the flashbang in the basement. My back aches from the metal chair. My ankles hurt from the chains. And of course my side still aches from the bullet wound, but none of it hurts as much as my heart.

I'm connected to the metal table in front of me by two lengths of chain. I think this is meant to convince me that the people who brought me here are not all bad. Same goes for the day-old sludge in the Styrofoam cup I keep cradled in my hands. It's something to hold on to.

The man stops tapping his fingers and takes a chair on the other side of the table. He looks like he belongs here, in this concrete room. I belong anywhere else.

I belong with Elijah.

I have a sinking feeling that he could be close. That should make me feel better, because if he's close then there's a chance I can get to him.

But if they have me chained to a desk, what are they doing to him? This could be one of a hundred concrete rooms all used for varying and terrible purposes. My pulse pounds. Would it be better or worse if I could hear his voice right now?

"Elijah North is a traitor." The man on the other side of the table drags a fingernail across the pitted metal surface. "That much we already know. We've been tracking his movements for some time, but it may come as a surprise to you. I understand you were… close."

He says this, and then he waits.

And waits.

The coffee trembles in the cup, though I could swear I'm staying still. There's nothing else to do. I'm chained to a table. Pulling at the chain isn't going to do anything but give away how much each passing second weighs on me.

It's a stupid weight, too. I shot one guy. That doesn't mean I can topple the U.S. government. The military. Especially with no weapons and lacking even the ability to stand up.

In the silence I can stay still, and I can listen for Elijah, and I can be afraid of what I might hear.

It goes on forever.

I clear my throat.

What does he want me to say? Yes, we were close. When he burst into the basement I wasn't wearing any pants, and I can still feel the fullness from when Elijah was inside me. Clearly we were close, but I don't know what the right answer is.

I'm going to burst out of my skin. That would put a wrench in his plans. The energy making itself at home in my nerves feels dangerous and raw and completely at odds with the fact that my options are down to two: answer or don't.

I stay silent. I'm listening for Elijah with so much focus that it feels like a knife through my temples. Like a bullet through my brain.

A sigh. "I want to help you, Holly, but you have to understand, this is a very serious charge. Whatever he told you, you need to let go of that. He was lying, probably."

"He's not a traitor." My voice sounds flat and contrary and as soon as the words are out in the air a new fear strikes. "And neither am I."

Maybe I don't understand what's really happening here.

Maybe the choices aren't what I think they are.

There's not enough time to think it through, because the man across from me straightens. The movement is so deliberate that I know he's relieved. He's been waiting for me to say something so he can continue with his job. "Do you know what treason is, Holly?"

"He didn't try to overthrow the government."

"That's a big word, overthrow." He's trying to look sincere, this guy. Trying to look like he means what he says, with the corners of his mouth turned down and his eyes on me like I'm a difficult student and not literally chained to the table. "I'm not sure that's what Elijah North did. But did he take money from the wrong people? Yes. Did he trust the wrong people? Yes."

He trusted me. "I don't believe you."

He folds his hands in front of him. "Evidence doesn't lie."

"I explained to you what happened with the colonel." I didn't break my promise to Elijah, not really. I did say that he shot the colonel, but I also explained that it was self defense. That the colonel was hounding him through France and Italy, that he refused to let him go. That he was going to use me as a pawn to get Elijah to obey him.

"If a foreign agency paid him to assassinate the colonel—"

That's the word they've been using. *Assassinate.* As if the colonel was some high-ranking political leader who was targeted by extremists. I can't prove that there wasn't a political agenda unless I admit that I shot the colonel, and that would break my promise. "It was self defense."

"He didn't only betray his country."

It takes effort not to crush the styrofoam cup. I know what he's going to say. I should have known this whole time. I should have stayed silent.

"He betrayed you, too. He's doing it as we speak."

"Really?" I've already given enough of myself to this man and all the others who took me away from Elijah. "Is that true? Tell me how. Give me every last detail."

"He told us that you were the one behind the plot. That you shot the colonel."

A weird, high laugh escapes me. He's trying to scare me, and the strange part is, it's working. Not because I believe him. I don't. My faith in Elijah has never been more sure, but it's terrifying to realize how easily the U.S. government can lie. "I don't believe you. You won't give me the details, you won't show me where he is. You won't take me to him."

He barely manages to keep himself from rolling his eyes.

For a heartbeat he looks like a bug, staring at me so he won't slump down in his seat and groan at how tedious this all is. It would be a relief, in a way, for this situation to be boring and commonplace and not an enormous victory for them.

Well, they already got Elijah. They got me, and I couldn't stop them. I'm not going to give them anything else.

I don't let myself think about the ways they might take it from me. My teeth ache from clenching them together. I want to repeat myself. Damn those old, people-pleasing instincts. I don't do it.

"Fine." He stands up and looms over me. Worry whispers over the place where my spine meets my skull. "If you won't tell me about Elijah, maybe your sister will be more forthcoming. They've met, haven't they?"

Fear runs cold over my skin. "You don't know anything about my sister."

He gives a slight grimace. "And I'd love to leave her out of it, but how can I do that when you won't cooperate with me? I need answers,

Holly, one way or another."

"I thought Elijah was already talking. You said that. That he was betraying me. So why do you need answers from me, too?"

Annoyance flashes through his eyes. He doesn't like that I've caught him in his own web, but he recovers quickly enough. "He's busy spinning a story in the room next door. He wants us to believe that it's all your fault, that you're some kind of international spy, but I don't believe that, Holly. I don't. I think you're just a girl who got caught up in a bad situation."

You could say that. I lived an ordinary life before this, but if I had never gotten on that plane to France, if I had never been kidnapped by Adam Bisset, I never would have found Elijah again. I'm not sure I would undo the past even if I could. "So if I'm just an ordinary girl in a bad situation, why am I sitting in chains right now?"

More annoyance. "I need answers. Understand?"

"You haven't asked a question."

"Who is Elijah North working for? Who gave him orders to kill the colonel?"

I swallow hard, knowing there's no way out of this. Elijah was right about that. He understood what was coming better than I did. They think there's some plot to take down the government, and it doesn't matter that they're wrong. We can never prove our innocence. It's an impossible task. Maybe I deserve to be free for shooting a person as despicable and violent as the colonel. Or maybe I deserve to be locked up for the rest of my life. I'm far more afraid that there's a different fate waiting for me, though. That's what Elijah was worried about. The low flickering lights make it feel like we're deep in a bunker somewhere. We drove far out of the city before getting here. No one knows where we are. Even if London had the resources to look for me, she wouldn't know where to start.

The easiest thing to do is simply make us disappear.

CHAPTER THIRTEEN
ELIJAH

THIS BEATING IS for amateurs.

If I was in charge of this and not Blue Shirt, I'd have built in some time for anticipation. These guys went right for the physical violence. That's a fine strategy, except for the fact that they didn't play any foundational mind games first. It's nothing but Holly, Holly, Holly and fists to the face. The electric shocks were an interesting twist but it turned out they got squeamish earlier than I would have.

The whole thing is taking too long.

My hands are behind my back again, and they've tipped the chair forward to kick my stomach from new angles. I've decided to start making more noise just so they think some progress is happening.

I would have taught them to do better.

I would have had the information inside an hour. It's about increasing the pain in slow increments, not battering a person until it's all the same to them whether they live or die.

Another knee connects below my ribs. This time the bloom of pain is different. Uh-oh.

Facts are facts: if someone hits you hard enough, for long enough, some internal bleeding is the result. There's a maximum limit that any one person can take. Another blow, this time directly on ribs, cracks one of them and interrupts my thought process. Oh, right—I don't have much time left.

At this rate, Blue Shirt is going to underestimate the damage and accidentally kill me.

Even so.

I bide my time until they let the chair fall backward. This is the second time my head has broken the fall and I feel it in my teeth. Let them think that a bruised skull is what finally makes me suck in a breath. "Okay. Okay, okay."

Blue Shirt looks like a demon with a halo. Disappointment flickers across his face. He's got his boot poised over my already-cracked rib. I resist the urge to roll my eyes. Over the course of our interrogation I've learned that the man is not actually Army but a Paramilitary Operations Officer with the CIA. His name is Joseph LeGrange, and his youngest wants a kitten for

Christmas. He's given me more information than I've given him.

He brings the boot down anyway and this time I taste copper. "I said okay, motherfucker."

"Pick him up."

The three of them maneuver me into an upright position. Zero points for creativity. Tipping over a fucking chair is effective, but it's not awe-inspiring. The only thing I've ever been awed by is Holly.

The prisoner's dilemma has one fatal flaw. Thinking of Holly reminds me of that. The prisoner's dilemma assumes both prisoners want the best deal for themselves. I don't want that. I've known from the minute they dragged me in here that I wasn't walking back out again. So a good deal for me is the least of my worries.

Holly's freedom is the only thing that matters.

The only thing.

I ignore the grasping, aching urge to touch her again and spend a few more moments pretending to compose myself. The one thing they haven't tried is offering to let me see her again. It strikes me as a huge oversight, but then again, Blue Shirt is an idiot.

"I shot the colonel." I keep my eyes on Blue Shirt's while I say it. He's the kind of fool who will take the eye contact at face value, even after all the fun time we've spent together. "I brought the gun to the apartment, planning to take that bastard out."

"That's not all you did." Blue Shirt rubs a hand over his knuckles and I swallow a sigh. I'm already confessing. Jesus Christ.

"Hell no. I kidnapped Holly." I let a big, crazy smile spread over my face, showing them bloody teeth. It's a half-genuine smile. Being with Holly at all, for any amount of time, is what makes this bearable. "I kidnapped her and I held her hostage."

A sneer curls the corner of his mouth. "You sick bastard."

"I raped her. So many times. She was my best victim." I think of her in the church. Before we drove away in the SUV. Before she decided to be a hero and shoot the colonel for me. Before that, I fucked her, hard and relentless, and she loved it. She was as pink and breathless as a doll when it was over. I focus on the feeling of my fingers between her legs. "It was an international crime. I raped her in several countries and forced her to cross the borders against her will. I forced her to do everything."

I want to lose myself in thinking of her. It's

too early for that. Saying a confession out loud is only the beginning of the act.

I clear my throat and it brings up fresh blood. Not the most positive sign, but I should have enough time left to do what I have to do to save her. "Write it up."

Blue Shirt narrows his eyes and glances over to his buddies. He looks like he wants to beat more confessions out of me. A goddamn hammer instead of a scalpel, this guy.

The government is getting sloppy, but it doesn't really matter. Not when you have billions of dollars in a defense budget and enough nukes to destroy the world ten times over.

Even sloppy wins.

"Write it up and I'll sign it." I taste more blood along with the words. It tastes like the truth. I'd sign anything if it means Holly lives. I'd sign anything to let her go free.

CHAPTER FOURTEEN

HOLLY

THE WATER HAS been running in the sink for so long that I've lost track of the time.

My kitchen sink. Running. The sound snaps me out of whatever reverie I've been in. At some point, I came over here to do something involving the sink. I turned on the water. Something caught my attention out the narrow kitchen window. It has a partial view of the alley next to the building, and a partial view of the street.

I don't know what I was looking at anymore.

Was it a white van that I saw or a postal truck? I have a hazy memory of both things. But, given the evidence of the sink, I'm not sure my memory is reliable at all.

I reach to turn off the water and find a mug in my hand. Right. That's why I came here. To pour out tea gone cold and clean the mug and put it in the rack to dry. My plan was thwarted by my still-constant search for Elijah.

He's gone.

There's no trace of him in my life. It's as if he never existed. As if I never hopped on a plane to France to find my sister. As if I never found him in the basement prison of a medieval church. All of it, erased.

Even the marks on my ass that perfectly matched his fingerprints have faded into nothing. I was sure they were there. I looked at them every day in the shower until they were gone.

I put coffee in the machine by the sink and set it to run. Now I'm the robot. I'm the one going through the ordinary movements of an ordinary life. It makes my skin crawl.

Everything about this life is fake, a facade, a charade. Or worse, everything that happened before was a hazard of imagination.

The part about being imprisoned by the government seems real enough. It ended with a knock on the door of the concrete room. The man who had been interrogating me walked out without a backward glance. Another man came in to unchain me from the table. He walked me to the back of the building, where a police car waited, and a cop who didn't speak to me drove me back to my apartment.

No *sorry about the part where we invaded a*

church and stole Elijah North from you. No apologies for chaining you to a table. It's protocol. You understand.

Nothing.

Nothing except the days I spent afterward, sobbing into my pillow and shouting into my phone. I was probably on a watch list before but I'm definitely on one now. I'm the crazed woman who sometimes puts on a serious voice as she inquires again and again if there is any way to contact Elijah North. If there are any personnel records for Elijah North. If there is any possible clue that he once existed. I've tried everything. I've tried lying. I've tried impersonating a reporter. I've tried letting my voice go thick and pretending to be his widow.

I tried for days, then weeks, then months.

The coffee brews and I stare out the window, actively searching for a white van now. Even if he did show up here, he wouldn't show up in a white van, but I can't stop looking. They're the symbol of my former life, aren't they? A white van brought me to him in the first place.

Search. Wonder. Pour the too-hot coffee into my clean mug. Wonder some more.

Is he dead?

If he's not dead, where is he?

There are so many days where it seems like I created him wholesale in my mind. It's not unheard of for a writer to feel like their characters are real people. This is different.

Elijah wasn't a character. Not one of mine, anyway. Which does call into question my general level of sanity.

A knock on the door pulls me away from the kitchen. I'm a ghost with hot coffee making my way through the apartment. There are quite a few takeout boxes on various surfaces.

I don't care.

I open the door without looking through the peephole. The worst that can happen is that I get kidnapped again, and what are the odds of that?

Not zero, certainly, but probably not very high at this point.

"Hi." My sister doesn't wait for me to answer before she pushes past me, her arms full of two paper grocery bags. "Did you eat today?"

"Yes," I say automatically, closing the door behind her. This might not be strictly true, but I can't remember. All I remember is standing in front of the sink. Earlier, I was writing. Or at least I was sitting on my couch, hand poised above a notepad.

The fridge opens and closes in the kitchen,

followed by several cupboards. I wander into the living room and look down at the street. No white vans there, either. Paper bags crinkle when London folds them up. In the window I see her reflection emerge from the kitchen carrying something black. A trash bag. She tips several of the takeout containers into it and straightens an abandoned stack of mail on my coffee table.

I swallow hard around a thickness in my throat. "Hey."

London flicks her eyes up to mine and continues tidying my apartment. "Hey."

"You're feeding me. And cleaning my apartment. It's weird."

She raises her eyebrows. "Yeah, it is weird, Holly. It's weird when you're acting like a dead person in your own apartment. It's weird when I'm the responsible one between us."

"Dead people don't leave takeout containers everywhere."

London gestures at me with a half-empty carton of Chinese food. "I never know what's going on with you. You don't even come out. It's like you've disappeared."

I snort. "I'm right here. The question is, what are *you* doing here?"

"I got worried when you didn't answer my

calls."

Turnabout is fair play, sure. I'm usually the one cleaning up after London. Following her to Paris. Getting her unstuck from shady diamond deals. So on, so forth. But I don't buy that she's worry-stricken enough to change her entire personality. Plus, I only missed three calls.

"What's going on with you?"

"You tell me first." She sticks out her tongue and goes out into the hall to put the garbage in the chute. "Anyway," she says, breezing back in. "You're the one who was detained by the government for questioning in an assassination."

"You're different," I tell her, and the moment I say it, I know it's true. "You look different."

"I look like I'm working a regular job. At a coffee shop. I'm taking a social media detox, which means no large influencer checks. Thanks so much for noticing."

It's not that. I study her more closely as she shakes out the blanket on my couch and lets it waft down over the back. It's accurate that she has less of an influencer shine on her. She's not as tan as she looks in her photos when she's traveling.

London looks good—she always looks good, because she's beautiful, but she looks comfortable, in a cream-colored sweater that sets off the red mark on her neck.

It looks like beard burn.

As if she's been with a man. Recently.

"Who is he?"

London's eyes go wide in a parody of surprise and her hand flutters toward the neck of the sweater. She catches herself just in time. "I don't know what you're talking about."

Two steps closer, and it's even easier to see the change in her skin. "Did you have a confrontation with a fir tree, London? Is that it? Or did you have some intense private time with a man? Judging from the state of your neck, he has stubble."

"What I do in my spare time is none of your business." My throw pillows are her next target. "You should be worried about yourself. I'm definitely worried about you."

"I'm fine. I'm more worried about your neck."

"My neck is fine."

"Who is he?"

She moves past me with a long-suffering energy. "I don't want to talk about it."

"So he's not hot."

A glare from London. "He is hot. And I don't want to talk about it."

"You, London Frank, do not even want to

talk about the sexy man who's all over you at night? I don't believe it. Talking about boys is your favorite thing. You used to talk about 'N Sync like they were your actual boyfriends. Come to think of it, I'm surprised you didn't become the author instead of me."

The coffee sloshes from the mug onto my hand. There's a beat when I don't feel the burn and then I do. I don't hate it. And I know that's not right.

A person shouldn't enjoy being burned by coffee, and I don't like it, not exactly. It's just that I remember so clearly what it felt like to hurt for someone else. For him.

London is staring at me with open concern on her face. "Your hand is turning red."

I wave my hand through the air, creating a breeze to cool the burn. "Tell me about the guy."

She looks away, then down. My sister's in the middle of my living room, shifting her weight from foot to foot, looking for the next thing to clean. It's been weeks of this habit. Bringing groceries. Picking up takeout containers. Folding my blanket. But it's the first time I've seen her with skin rubbed raw from stubble. London glances at my hand, which is the same shade of red. And then my face, which probably looks animated for the first time in weeks.

"It's a guy named Adam."

"Adam. Nice. Did you meet him at the coffee shop?" I laugh, and the sound is off somehow, but at least I'm doing it. At least I'm finding some amusement in talking to my sister, which is an improvement over a robotic existence. "I bet he slipped you his number on a napkin."

London meets my eyes, but she's worrying her bottom lip with her teeth, rubbing a hand along the back of her neck. It's not embarrassing to meet someone in a coffee shop.

Unless she didn't meet him in the coffee shop.

Unless the expression on her face is about more than a one-night-stand situation with a hot guy from the coffee shop.

"Adam." The word takes forever to leave my lips. "An Adam we already know?"

"Yeah."

I…can't. I can't process it, can't let it soak in, can't even let the information register for what seems like an eternity but is probably more like a minute. So many questions spring to mind.

Like how, and why, and when.

I'm too shocked to ask any of them.

What would the answers be, anyway? I feel an ancient urge to scold her, remind her about the dangers of being with men like Adam, but it would be laughably hypocritical.

London watches me turn into a statue of a woman holding coffee. "Holly."

"No. It's fine. Of course you can have sex with whoever you want."

"Holly."

"I'm not judging you. Just be careful, you know. Men like that." My voice breaks. "Men like that have a way of disappearing. As if they were never even real."

I break down sobbing and she holds me while I cry on her shoulder. Even her smell is different, some kind of masculine shampoo mixed with her own floral scent. I cry until I'm left with only hiccups and a throbbing head.

She kisses me on the forehead and leaves, promising to come back the next day. The door closes behind her. Sometime later I realize the coffee is gone. I drank it. I'm the only one here. There's nothing left but coffee grounds in the bottom of the cup, swirled into the shape of a fleur de lis. It's very French. But the coffee grounds aren't what I'm thinking about.

It's the beard burn on my sister's neck that has me transfixed.

That one red mark is proof.

I wasn't crazy.

If Adam exists, then so did Elijah.

And if he was alive, that means he could still be alive.

Please let him be alive.

If he's still alive, he needs me.

CHAPTER FIFTEEN

HOLLY

IT TAKES A full day to come up with an idea. I decide to put it into motion before lunch. London hasn't sent a single text since she left, but she did send takeout. As soon as it arrives I abandon it on the coffee table. Who can eat?

I can't wait any longer to make this phone call.

Google reveals plenty of references to North Security. There are a few images by the Associated Press of high-ranking politicians and celebrities with men wearing suits and dark sunglasses in the background. There are some news articles about new security technology with quotes from Joshua North, co-owner and spokesperson for the company.

There are a few magazine articles about the prodigy violinist Samantha Brooks and her budding romance with her bodyguard, a man who was once her guardian. Liam North. The oldest brother. The founder of North Security.

The call connects after half a ring. "North Security."

"Hi." I lean back on the couch, the details of my plan disappearing like a mermaid into deep water. My hands are shaking. This is just a phone call, but my body won't settle down. "I'm calling to speak with Liam North."

Despite having lots of references elsewhere, the company website is sparse. A white background, a sleek logo, and an email address. There are no flashy images or little reassurances in text to make a prospective client want to call. I get the impression they're massively successful both in private security and government contracts, but it must come through referrals.

"He's not available right now. You can leave a message with—"

"No." The startled silence on the other end of the line is the first clue this woman doesn't get interrupted often. "I mean—it's an urgent call."

"Mr. North receives many urgent calls in the course of business. If you'll leave your name and number, I'll pass along a message." She's already started typing again, fast and loud.

"I need to speak with him." For some reason, for some stupid reason, I thought this part of the phone call would be the easy part. "Right now. There's a security problem. A bad one." Very smooth, Holly. Very believable. I can hear my heartbeat thudding like a hammer on concrete. "I need to hire North Security for a private security job."

"Again, miss, you're welcome to leave a message with—"

"It's about his brother," I say flatly. "Elijah."

"One moment, please."

Apparently Elijah's name was the magic word. There's a brief pause. The phone doesn't have a chance to ring before Elijah's brother is on the line. "I wasn't expecting a call from you, Holly." His voice is so like Elijah's that it crushes my heart and makes it hard to breathe.

"How did you know it was me?"

"We have caller ID."

A manic laugh bursts from me. "Oh. Of course. Yes. Not because you're fancy security people. Even though you are. The article in Vanity was really impressive."

"Tell me what happened."

So I tell Liam North what happened. I tell him about the meeting with my editor from a thousand years ago, missed because of Elijah. I tell him about the church hideout and Adam. About the colonel. About the gun. About getting shot. He says less and less after this until finally he's dead silent while I tell him about the raid and my subsequent release and the horrible absence in my life since then, and how I am looking for his brother, and how I need his help.

The silence stretches on until I can't take it anymore. I already feel wrung out from telling the story in the first place and the worry that's held me in its grip since the church.

"Did we get disconnected?"

"No."

"You're going to help him, right?"

There's a soft shuffling in the background, as if he's rifling through papers. "Don't get involved in this, Holly. Forget Elijah. Pretend you've never met him."

The words register first. Then the shock. Then a clean, hot fury. "How dare you. He loves you." I leap up from the couch and pace through my living room, trying and failing to work out the urge to reach through the phone and strangle Liam.

He's turning his back on his brother, and why? Why?

"You can't save him."

"The hell I can't."

He sighs. "The things you're talking about, they're above your pay grade. They're above *my* pay grade. If Elijah made an enemy of a dirty colonel then there's going to be a lot of people interested in his death. Not only the government, but whoever he had illegal ties to. You can't protect him against that, Holly. Leave it alone."

There's a click. He's hung up.

It's not until I've thrown the phone into a couch cushion that I discover the tears slipping down my cheeks. The takeout container seems like a cruel joke now. How am I supposed to sit here and eat when Elijah was real, he could be alive, and even his brothers won't help me? Bile rises in my throat. Forget the food. Forget everything.

I reach for the phone to send a text to London. It's something to do, even if it won't solve the problem, and I can't be here alone with this. Not completely.

My fingers freeze over the keyboard.

I'm not thinking.

It's not because I was about to text London for comfort, either. My brain has been in a fog since yesterday because of what she told me. Because she told me that she's seeing Adam.

And I sat on that information for a full day,

then put all my hopes in Liam North's basket.

My winter jacket feels enormous on my frame but I zip myself into it, put on a hat, and leave my apartment for the first time in weeks.

It takes fifteen minutes in an Uber to get to London's apartment, and then it's three floors up. I'm burning up inside the jacket by the time I'm pounding my fist against the door.

"London. I need your help."

It's insane that we haven't talked about this. Sure, yes, it would be hypocritical to fight with her about the fact that she's with my original kidnapper, but a good sister would at least ask. A good sister would press for the details before she leverages that man for everything he's worth.

The deadbolt disengages on the other side and the door opens.

I'm not surprised to see Adam on the other side. I knew he was with her in some capacity, but to see him standing here sends a wave of indignation tearing through me. That, and the fact that he's in a pair of low-slung sweatpants and nothing else. "Are you living here?"

"For the moment." Adam ushers me inside and it is irritating, it is infuriating, how easily he does it. He looks completely at home in the cluttered, bohemian apartment.

"Where's my sister?"

"I'm right here." London steps out of the bathroom in a t-shirt and leggings with a towel around her hair, looking wide-eyed and wary. "Are you okay?"

"Are *you* okay?" I cross my arms over my chest and stare at her. "You told me you were seeing him. You didn't say you shacked up with him. He kidnapped me."

"For what it's worth, I am sorry about that," Adam puts in.

London holds up both her hands. "It didn't seem like the best time to mention—"

"That this man is living in your apartment? Living here, London, not just dating you, not just hooking up with you, living here. What were you thinking?" London and Adam exchange a glance, which pisses me off even more. "Oh, so it wasn't you. It was Adam's idea."

"There were extenuating circumstances," he says.

I stab a finger in his general direction, cutting off whatever pointless explanation he's about to give me. "Elijah is in danger. He's going to be tried for treason—or worse."

"Why should I care?" He puts a hand to his side and drops it. "Last time I saw him, he shot me."

"Because you deserved it. And also he let you leave."

Adam sighs. "Look. It's complicated. The colonel has too much power for one man. I know that more than anyone, but that doesn't change the reality. He's too strong to beat."

The colonel, the colonel. If I never have to hear another word about the colonel it will be too soon. "Not exactly. He's dead."

I've never seen Adam look so surprised. I wasn't sure he was even capable of this expression. He looks...stunned. "What? No. What the fuck did you just say? He's not dead."

"Oh yes." I give him a sharp nod. "He's really dead. I shot him myself."

Adam sits down heavily on the couch, his hands folded under his chin, and without his shirt he looks somehow like a lost little boy despite the large muscles and three days of scruff. "That changes everything. Jesus Christ. The colonel. Dead. Shot by a civilian."

"It changes nothing." My voice is so sharp it's cutting my throat and bringing burning tears to my eyes. "I did it to save Elijah, but it only made things worse."

He frowns. "How is it worse?"

"Because now the U.S. government thinks he did some kind of treason plot. They think he was paid by a foreign country or something."

"But you're the one who shot him."

I swallow around the knot in my throat. "Yes."

His solemn eyes meet mine. "You should leave it alone. Elijah sacrificed himself for you. This is how he'd want it."

"No, damn it." Adam blinks at the raw edge of my voice. "I refuse to give up on him. He never gave up on me."

CHAPTER SIXTEEN

ELIJAH

I HAVE NO explanation for the airport hanger.

It's a change of scenery, at least. No more cinder block walls. Only massive ceilings coated in fireproof sealant foam. The sound of fists hitting flesh echoes off those high ceilings while a new set of henchmen take turns with me. Possibly they're just using me for practice. Someone has to be the test dummy for torture school, after all.

I've had just enough recovery time to be conscious for this latest session. Lucky me.

They've been at it for fifteen minutes or so when a door opens at the other side of the room and a man in a suit and overcoat walks in like he's late for a board meeting. One of the Army men makes a show of pulling out a chair for him, which he takes.

"Don't stop on my account."

One of them drives a fist through my gut all the way to my spine and steps back to let me finish coughing. The man in the suit stays far enough away that drops of blood just miss his shiny black shoes. He's wearing a suit that probably costs as much as a damned private jet.

"Good evening," he says, not sounding disgusted in the least to see me hanging here like dried meat. "You don't know me, but I've been watching you for many years."

"Well, that's creepy."

He adopts an amused expression. "You got your orders from the colonel, but did you ever wonder where he got his orders?"

"Let me guess. From you."

"You always were a smart boy. I think I understood that even better than the colonel. You knew someone had to be pulling his puppet strings, but you knew better than to ask questions." He frowns. "You were so useful, for so long. Perhaps we took you for granted."

"Are you supposed to be the good cop?"

A low laugh. "Compared to bruiser here? No. I don't speak with my fists, but neither am I the one who's going to coddle you. I'm the person who controls the board. I move the pieces around. And until very recently, you were one of my pieces."

Until Holly Frank appeared in that prison cell

with me. Everything changed in that moment, no matter how hard I fought it. "You never controlled me."

"Every creature likes to believe he's in charge of his own fate."

I was in charge of my own fate. Holly taught me that. She shot the colonel to free me, but it was her example that truly unleashed me. She didn't flinch in the face of guns, in the face of danger. Holly, a woman with no military training. It was the same thing she did for her sister, hopping on the plane for France. She's fearless. "I did what you said because it suited me. It suited me to be mindless and violent, and I let you use me. Probably to do shit that was far more traitorous and harmful to my country than shooting the colonel."

"Traitorous." He looks offended. "What I do may not be sanctioned by the upper echelons of military personnel, but it's what keeps this country afloat. They don't understand the big picture. For them it's all about duty and regulations. The enemy doesn't care about those things."

"The enemy being... who? Me?"

A small smile. "You can't play stupid with me."

I hang my head, too fucking exhausted to care. "Let me guess. You think someone paid me to kill the colonel. North Korea or Russia or something like that."

"Of course not, don't be foolish. We have ties with North Korea and Russia. They may have harsh, dictatorial regimes, but they understand the chain of command. I appreciate that about them. No, I'm worried about a threat a little closer to home."

A snarl breaks out of me. "Don't tell me this has anything to do with Holly Frank."

"Was that her name? I heard you got led around by your dick. Tits and ass will bring even the strongest man down." He holds out his hands in question. "But how can I judge? I'm not immune. It's the weakest part of our nature."

She's the strongest part of me. "And your point?"

"You want to protect the woman. That's very chivalrous of you, but no, I don't particularly care about her. You think I'm here to torture you, to kill you."

I look down at my battered body. "It's a decent guess."

He smiles. "What do you do when a fifty thousand dollar diamond necklace breaks? Do you throw the whole thing away? Of course not. You have it repaired. You are far too valuable for me to kill you. What a waste that would be."

"Fuck you."

The Army men don't like my tone. They express their displeasure by working as a team. One of them holds my head back by my hair while another one digs his fingers hard into the sides of my neck. It doesn't take very long for the blood supply to get cut off. It takes almost no time for my vision to go dark at the edges. He keeps it up until my breath strangles.

When he lets go the air tastes fresh and clean.

The man in the suit stands across from me, watching this with a detached disinterest. "How did the colonel communicate with you?"

"I can't remember."

That earns me a blow from one of his minions.

"No, wait. I've got it. We communicated via carrier pigeon."

It's stupid and it's reckless and I know it. I know I should pretend to take his questions seriously. The problem is that everything hurts and I want this to be over. It's exhausting to be constantly tortured. I'd put up with it every day for the rest of my life if it meant guaranteeing

Holly's safety. So as long as she's not part of this, then I'll play my role. They're making her part of it.

My friends from the CIA circle around like wolves around a corpse.

One of them steps forward to hit me again, but the man with perfect shoes holds up his hand.

"Give us a few minutes alone."

"But, sir—" Their ringleader steps up to the side of the guest of honor's chair, genuine confusion on his face. "This man is a highly trained operative. Are you sure—"

"He's tied up, starved, and beaten to within an inch of his life." Our newest arrival adjusts one of his sleeves. "As long as you guys have been doing your jobs, I have nothing to worry about, do I? Now leave."

In the answering silence the torture squad files out in a neat row.

"So," I say when we're alone. "You gonna tell me who the fuck you are? Because I know you're not military. No one in the ranks can afford that tie."

He looks smug. "Why would I trust you with that information?"

"You want me to work for you, right? That means I'll have to know who you are. Besides the fact that if you don't like what I say, you can put a bullet between my eyes."

"You can call me the senator."

"Is that supposed to be ironic? Like you're actually in the House of Representatives, so we call you the senator to throw them off the scent?"

The senator straightens his jacket, frowning down at me. He looks fucking terrifying. Like a man possessed. I'm not sure if I can feel appropriate levels of fear, except when it comes to Holly. I shouldn't be afraid of this guy at all, but there's a glint in his eyes I don't like. "This woman," he says. "She can be yours. Tied up in a penthouse suite whenever you get back from a mission. Whatever you want. You were underpaid before. Underappreciated. That changes now."

"I prefer to do my own kidnapping, but thanks."

"Women. Money. Anything you want can be yours if you work for me."

"I think you might be getting ahead of yourself." I flex my fingers so they don't fall off from being restrained behind my back. "People are going to look into the colonel's business now that he's dead. People will find out that the two of you were connected. Maybe they'll ask questions. I could probably help them connect a few dots."

He grits his teeth, and for the first time since he entered the room I've gotten under his skin. I rotate my wrists around in the bonds to see if the rope loosens up.

It doesn't.

The senator is openly scowling. Openly hating the fact that I remember things from a time other than now. He strides toward me, eating up the distance between us in four long steps. But he doesn't stop when it would be normal. He stops right in front of me and reaches down to the front of my pants.

"What the fuck—"

The sentence dies mid-thought because he squeezes. The senator is crushing the life out of my balls. They feel flattened. Irredeemable. I'm never going to be able to repair the damage he's done. This is for Holly. All of this is for Holly. Remember that.

He twists, and pain explodes across my belly. It's punctuated by the senator laughing. "If I get my hands on your girl," he says. "I'm going to fuck her until she bleeds from her pussy."

I focus on breathing through my gritted teeth. Fuck, I'm angry. I'm so angry, and it hurts to be here. There's one way to make it hurt less.

I let my eyes close, then murmur something

unintelligible.

The senator leans in closer. "What was that?"

"Fuck you," I tell him.

"Remember." His forehead is inches from mine. "Remember what just came out of your mouth, asshole. Remember that when I'm reaming your pretty little girlfriend in the ass."

I mumble again, and the senator can't resist. He just can't. He leans in even closer, struggling to understand me and probably hoping to have me shot right now.

That's when I snap my head forward and slam my forehead into the senator's head. He reels back, sitting down hard on the floor and sucking in deep breath after deep breath.

My own head hurts.

It hurts like a bitch.

Like a cracked skull. A dying star.

He's still down there when I maneuver the rope around my wrists into a position where I can leverage my own body weight to get it off. By the time I'm freed from the goddamn steel chair, the senator is coming around to regular consciousness. He gets his feet under him, eyes searching for the door, but I haul him up higher.

It gives me the perfect positioning for an effective choke hold.

The senator, it turns out, doesn't have a lot of experience being in a choke hold. He doesn't struggle nearly enough. A few halfhearted swipes at my arms and face and he's already going limp in my arms. When his head falls to the side I drop him to the floor.

There's nothing to do but run.

Airport hangers are built with several exits, so I take the one the Army men didn't use.

The cold air slams into me like a living god that's pissed at me. Being outside is a shock to the system. A blistering return to reality. I'm out here anyway.

With no shoes and no shirt and a deep constellation of bruises all over my body. I'm covered in blood. I must look like a nightmare.

But even nightmares have places to be.

It's at least twenty miles to New York City. The light pollution acts as a beacon. Icy cold seeps in through the soles of my feet. It's only going to get worse when I leave the concrete pad that supports the airport hanger. One step into the snow proves me right. It's goddamn freezing.

I'm never going to make it.

Two steps and I know I'm going to lose some toes.

I'll make it, but maybe not in one piece.

Ten steps and the pain is like knives. Moving hurts. Stepping in the snow hurts. Keeping my eyes open hurts.

I keep them open anyway.

I'm going to find her.

CHAPTER SEVENTEEN

HOLLY

A DAM STARES OUT the window of London's apartment for a long time.

Then he rubs both hands over his face and lets out a long, tortured breath. "It's traitors all the way down, Holly. The colonel had a chain of command, too. Someone was giving him orders."

"Fine. Who's above him?" Something important inside me has snapped. London has Adam here, for god's sake. That's at least as dangerous as being around Elijah, so I don't buy this bullshit that I should stay away for my own safety. "Give me a name."

"It's not so simple." Adam's eyes flicker over to London, who is still standing by her bedroom with a towel around her hair.

She looks from Adam to me and back again. "I'm going to get dressed."

"Good idea." It's an asshole tone to take with her but I am at the end of my rope. Later I'll have to deal with the fact that I am pissed at her for not telling me about Adam the moment he showed up in her apartment. It's clear from the way he answered the door that he didn't arrive ten minutes ago. He's been here. London disappears into her bedroom and closes the door.

"Give me a name." My spine feels like steel on fire. If there's one thing I'm not going to do, it's walk out of this apartment without getting anything out of Adam. He owes me this. *Sorry about kidnapping you* isn't going to cut it. "Or I swear to god, Adam."

Before he put me in that first white van, it might have been an empty threat. Back then I didn't know how to shoot a gun and wouldn't have had the balls to get one and use it. Now I'm willing to do anything. Anything. Up to and including threaten my former kidnapper.

He doesn't laugh. My face must be proof of my new take-no-prisoners attitude.

The light in the room changes. We're heading toward late afternoon and fast. It'll be full dark by six. I don't care if it gets dark. All I care about is taking another step forward. I won't know the shape of the game until I can feel the walls caging us in.

"There's a fundraiser tonight."

I want to strangle him for this until I realize he's not telling me that he has another engagement or that we should attend for altruistic reasons. Of course he isn't. This is Adam. Adrenaline injects itself into my veins and makes the tips of my fingers throb.

"It's an event that attracts a lot of key players."

I still don't see how this gets us to Elijah. "What are you suggesting we do? Poison their champagne?"

A grin ghosts across Adam's face. "We use the powers of pointed conversation to pull the strings of the web."

"And once we find him?"

He sobers. "Then we'll know if Elijah can be saved or if it's too late."

A lump in my throat gives a painful twist and I swallow against it. "It's not too late. Let's go to the fundraiser."

"What fundraiser?" London cuts in. She's back from her bedroom, her hair in a bun that still manages to look elegant even with wet hair. "You can't go to a fundraiser looking like you've been hiding in your apartment for weeks. Plus, why?" She takes us both in, suspicion in her eyes. "Why would you leave now?"

"To save a man who doesn't want to be

saved," Adam says. "I owe him one for not shooting me through the heart."

"To confront the people who have taken him *hostage*," I point out. "It's illegal, what they're doing, and probably torture—"

"You can't," London says simply. "You know you can't."

"There are no other options." Adam is being so calm and soothing that I could die. "It's risky. It's dangerous. I can't lie to you about that. You should walk away."

"So you're telling me there are dangerous people at this fundraiser." London purses her lips, eyes flashing. "You're telling me that my sister will be around them, poking at them."

"Oh, yes. Many. Several who might not be pleased to see me."

"You're not doing it, then. You're not taking my sister into *another* dangerous place."

"Yes, he is," I say, at the same time Adam says "Yes, I am."

"You—" London's chin quivers. "You've been hiding here. You've been hiding here *because they could kill you*. I won't let you drag my sister back into harm's way."

"He's not dragging me. And if you're going to stand here and fight with me, then I'll just leave.

I'll go by myself. Looking like this, if I have to." Every heartbeat is another second that Elijah could be hurt, or dying. "I have to do this, London."

Adam and London exchange a look. I hate them for this look. I hate that they're in a position to exchange a look at all and I'm here without Elijah and without my heart.

"I'll need clothes, too," Adam says. "We'll meet back here in two hours."

"Don't do this," London says, her voice low and strained.

Adam pauses.

London swallows hard. "I'm asking you not to."

I can't take a breath while I wait for Adam's verdict.

Adam drops his chin to his chest. "And any other time, I'd listen to you. Order me around in bed, please. Tell me what to do with my fucking life. I'm game. But not this. If there's a chance to expose the colonel for what he was, I'm going to take it, even if it means losing you."

Adam gives London a last, lingering look, and then he's gone.

London drops her head into her hands.

"I'm sorry." It's not enough, but it's all I have

left to give her. I pull my purse close. "I have to go."

"Oh, shut up, Holly." She lifts her head and her cheeks are flushed, eyes red. Crying over *Adam*? If this were a normal day, I'd make her sit on the couch with a bottle of wine and tell me what the hell is going on. But she's already in motion, grabbing her purse and searching for her coat. "I know a salon that can help you. They're good in an emergency."

"Are you sure?"

"Don't ask me that again. Just follow me."

I have my doubts about the emergency hair salon, but it turns out my sister is right. They are good in an emergency. An hour after we walk in, my hair has been cut and styled and they've put on enough makeup to hide my pale skin and the smudges under my eyes. With an hour to go before the fundraiser, London walks quickly back down the block. I keep up without asking questions as she makes one turn, then another, then tells me to wait outside the door of a boutique. She comes out a minute later with a garment bag slung over her shoulder.

We do not discuss Adam.

The apartment is still empty when we come back. Thirty minutes to go. She hustles me into the bedroom and starts pulling out all the necessary pieces to strap me into a cocktail gown.

I should have given her more credit. I wasn't aware until I sat down at the salon what a mess I've become, but in twenty minutes flat London has me taped into a gown and slipping on heels. She rifles through her closet, picking out a purse that goes.

"You look good," she says.

"I look like shit."

"You feel like shit." London is very sage. "But you're beautiful."

I give her a hug. A big one. She's partially responsible for the worst of everything that's happened, but she's also the reason I met Elijah again. "I love you, London. You know that, right? You're my best sister."

It's something I said to her when we were little. She gives me a wry smile, because she's my only sister. Even if I had a hundred, London would be my best sister. I would fly to the ends of the earth to protect her, and I'm so grateful she's fought the addiction this hard.

We step out of the bedroom and find Adam waiting in the living room. He looks like a different man than the scruffy, shirtless hottie who was here earlier. Now he's in a suit, looking like he belongs at a masquerade ball in a castle in Italy.

I'm the one who's had a hasty emergency makeover, but Adam only has eyes for London.

"When do you think you'll be back?" She reaches over and smooths a panel of my dress.

"Not too late," says Adam. There's apology in his voice.

It's such a mundane, normal thing to ask and a mundane, normal answer that tears sting the corners of my eyes. I'm not going to let them fall. Not with all this makeup on. But jealousy is a pair of rough hands cracking ribs. "Okay," I say, taking the clutch purse from London. "Let's go find Elijah North."

✧   ✧   ✧

THE FUNDRAISER IS held at a fancy hotel because of course it is. This is probably our only lucky break. Adam escorts me in through the front doors. We pretend to head for the check-in desk at the lobby, then change course, meandering toward the enormous ballroom along the back of the hotel. Soft music makes a backdrop for the swells of powerful people talking.

We get rid of our coats at the coat check, and then it's time to go in.

The party could be the same one London and I went to in that Italian castle several lifetimes ago. It's the same scene, different setting. Men in dark suits. Women in jewel-toned dresses. Bubbling drinks and subtle decorations and the thick scent of money.

My stomach drops. There are too many people in here, and if Adam is right, then any one of them could be the one who's keeping Elijah from me. Any one of them could be the person who was controlling the colonel. The U.S. government is a hydra. Cut off one head, and another one grows in its place.

Adam puts a steadying hand on the small of my back. "Think of it as window shopping."

"Seriously?"

"We're just looking for anything that stands out."

I want to laugh, but if I start, I might not stop. So I press my lips together and follow Adam into the fray.

I'm bracing myself to fake small talk with one of the other women fluttering around the room when someone jostles Adam. Another man in a suit. He turns around with a practiced smile on his face. "My apologies—I didn't see you there. I'm Senator Ewan York."

Adam shakes his hand without missing a beat and gives a fake name for both of us.

The senator has a nasty bruise on his forehead, and he sees me looking. "Oh, that. A skiing accident. They call them double black diamonds for a reason."

Adam laughs, and the senator goes on to tell us how a near-miss on the slopes resulted in him going headfirst into buried ice. "Oh, no," I hear myself say. "I'm glad you were all right."

The senator's eyes light on me. "The company of a beautiful woman could speed up the healing process. Perhaps you'd let me tell you about my new clean air initiative."

Every inch of my skin crawls, but I force myself to put on a smile. In this room of people with perfect spray tans and perfect clothes, the bruise is an ugly departure. "I could use a drink and some conversation."

Adam seems distracted. Bored enough to let the senator "steal me away" for a trip to the bar. He offers me his elbow and I take it, stomach turning. He tells me more about his ski trip while we approach the bar and he orders two of the signature drinks. All of the details are surface level, like he read a Wikipedia article about tourism in Aspen.

I'm nearing old age when he reaches the end of his story. "What brings a woman like you to our little party tonight? I haven't seen you at one of these fundraisers before."

I wave a hand next to my head, murmur something about how loud it is, and steer us toward one of the exits. "Oh, that's better," I say in the open air of the hallway. Several smaller ballrooms line the hall, all of them dark, and I pretend to choose a direction at random. The farther we are from the rest of these people, the better. "I came here to meet a friend of a friend."

The senator has put his hand low on one of my hips, and he slowly works it around to my back. "Is this friend of a friend destined to remain a secret?"

"He knew someone I met through...complicated circumstances." I frown a little, to show him this might be difficult to talk about, and lean toward one of the empty ballrooms. The senator comes willingly. He moves us into the cut of light from the ballroom door, still letting me hover on the edge of safety. "A certain colonel who recently met a bad end."

His eyes turn mean and dark, a fist clenching by his side. "Who the hell are you?"

"My real name is Holly Frank."

"So you're the tits and ass."

My eyes narrow. "What a gentleman. I'm sure your constituents would be thrilled to know they elected a person like you. Maybe we should go out there and tell them what you're really like."

"My constituents don't give a fuck how I treat little sluts like you."

That's probably not an amazing sound bite for him, but I'm not satisfied with a comment that some news sites won't even air. I want a full confession. "Elijah told me all about you. How you gave orders to the colonel, how you're going to find another Army front man now that he's dead. I know everything."

A smirk. "Another Army front man? I have twenty, sweetheart. In every goddamn government department and agency. When one falls down, another stands in his place."

I shiver at the menace in his voice. "You don't need to worry about Elijah North. You worry about me. I'm the one who knows your secrets."

"If you know a single thing about me, you know that I could shoot you right where you stand. And I could get away with it. That's my power."

I pull my phone out of my clutch, pressing the *pause* button on the record app. "That just got uploaded to the cloud, by the way. So I hope you're ready to answer questions about that."

His eyes narrow. "You little bitch."

My heart is ready to leap out of my body and sprint for the lobby. But instead of leaving, instead of abandoning me to this empty room and his threats, he plants his feet. The senator blocks the door.

The hallway isn't empty anymore. There are shadows out there, suited shadows, and in a rush of shame I realize how foolish I've been. Of course he would come here with people.

Of course he wouldn't say all those things to me and let me live.

I'm trapped.

CHAPTER EIGHTEEN

ELIJAH

SHE'S NOT AT her apartment, and I'm a human train wreck.

I pound on the door one more time. "Holly, answer me."

There's nothing but silence on the other side. No hint of a person avoiding me. No lights on, no TV on, nothing. No sign that she's alive. What if they never let her go? What if she's been tied to a chair like me for weeks? What if she died during one of the torture sessions?

I force the lock. It's pathetic, and if she ever comes back here again I will personally come change the damn thing, but my suspicions are confirmed. Holly's gone.

Fear cuts into my already bruised belly.

The confession I made was to free her, which means she should be here. In a city like this, there are a million reasons to leave your apartment. Doesn't matter. Something's off. Something's wrong. She's an author, for god's sake. She works from home; she should be here.

I search through the unopened mail and take-out receipts until I find one with another address scribbled on it. Sushi, enough for two women to eat. It could be a loose lead, but I'm betting this will take me to her sister.

The trip to London's apartment is as excruciating as the twenty-mile trek back into the city. The stolen shoes don't fit my feet, and my skin bleeds from the rough terrain. I found a replacement shirt with long sleeves but no new pants. It explains the strangled gasp London makes when she opens her door. "What happened to you?"

"You shouldn't be so quick to undo the lock. You never know who'll be out here."

London beckons me inside. It's not necessarily a good idea to invite a guy like me into her apartment, but she's determined, scanning the hallway in both directions before she shuts the door behind us. "Holly has been worried sick about you. Literally."

Guilt burns a path through frozen skin. "Where is she?"

"She went to look for you."

"What do you mean?" My blood runs cold at the thought of her in some Army office, asking questions that will get her in trouble. Or worse, in an airport hangar somewhere.

"There was some event. I told her not to go. I told her it was dangerous. But does anyone listen to me? No. I'm not even going to talk to Adam ever again."

"Wait. Adam was here?"

"Yeah, I know you two have some kind of beef, but he seemed really shook up about the colonel being dead. He said that changed everything."

"It does change everything. The colonel was Adam's father."

"What?"

"Where is this event?"

"It's some fundraiser at a hotel with some big shot senator."

Some senator. Jesus. I head for the door. "I'm going to kill that bastard for letting her step foot in that hotel. I'm going to do it right now."

"I don't think so." London puts her body between me and the door, which is probably the most dangerous thing she's ever done. It's like standing between a caged lion and the exit. It's asking to get her head crushed. "It's some black-tie fundraiser."

"And?"

"And you'll never get through the door looking like a busted-up mountain man. Is that blood on your pants? Is it possible you were mauled by a bear on your way here? You look terrible."

"I don't care."

"Yeah, no. Get in the shower. I'll get you some clothes."

I normally don't take orders from people like London Frank, but I can't argue with her assessment. The shower is heaven and hell all at once. The hot water is heaven. The water on the scrapes and cuts is hell. Washing my hair is heaven. Putting my hands above shoulder level is hell. Life is a tapestry of bullshit.

The shower takes time I don't have. When I come out of the bathroom London is waiting with menswear slung over one arm. I don't even ask where she found a tux in her cardboard box of an apartment. "I think it'll fit," she says, eyes skimming over the cuts and bruises on my torso. "Are you sure you shouldn't be going to a hospital?"

"Give me the clothes."

I climb into them piece by piece, London standing by like a dressing room attendant. There's a moment when I'm pulling the undershirt over my head that my cracked rib protests and I freeze, letting the pain run its course.

"Jesus," she whispers.

"He had nothing to do with this."

I finish dressing in the suit and step back into the bathroom. The man in the mirror is unrecognizable, and it's not just because of the bruises on his face and the tight set of his jaw. I'm going to wear my teeth down to nubs if I don't get some painkillers soon. But more painful by far than the beating is being apart from Holly.

More painful than that is the possibility that by going after her, I could put her in more danger.

That's always been the way with us, hasn't it?

No use fighting.

London pokes her head in. "I called you a car. It's waiting outside."

"Thanks."

"You will protect Holly, won't you?"

With any luck Holly won't have gotten near the senator. Or maybe it's another senator. There are ninety-nine others, after all. But I have a sinking feeling about this. Adam would know more about his father's shady business than anyone else. If he's determined to help Holly, if he decided to try and find me, he would know where to start looking.

I have the driver make a single stop on the way to the hotel.

When I get there, the fundraiser is in full swing. No one looks twice at me as I move through the front doors. Every step is agony. It's not the long-distance walk that did so much damage, it was the fact that I did it after getting the shit beat out of me.

Even Dax wouldn't recommend a hike like that after a torture session.

I don't see Adam in the ballroom, which is my first clue that Holly's not where she's supposed to be. A few guys mill in a side hall, looking into an overflow room.

One of them says something to the others, and then they're on the move, heading quickly in the opposite direction.

I follow them.

Let this not be a distraction.

It's up a floor to the parking garage. Two of them split off, going up, and one jogs into the rows of cars and disappears.

"I'm not going with you." Holly's voice echoes off the concrete supports and my heart seizes. It's hard to tell which direction the sound is coming from so I start walking, trying to keep my footfalls light. "Let go of me."

I walk faster.

I find her at the end of the row, another man's hand locked around her upper arm. She has one palm braced on the frame of a car, the open door yawning next to her.

The senator increases the pressure on her arm and she cries out. "I'm still not going," she says, fighting but not getting very far. "Let me go. I'll scream."

"Scream, then." He's impatient and he looks even worse than the last time I saw him. "My men are all over this parking garage. There's no way in hell you're getting free."

I understand exactly how Holly felt at her apartment, the certainty that she felt when she shot the colonel, the determination to destroy everything that might hurt her. It's no surprise that I love Holly. I think I've loved her since Italy, since France. I've loved her since the first time I kissed her in Paris, but the shock is that she loves me.

She risked everything to save me. That's love.

I let out a battle cry and run toward them at full speed. The senator sees me. His eyes widen. He tries to turn so that Holly will be his human shield, but she chooses that moment to jab him in the stomach with her elbow. It keeps him off balance, and I throw him against the car. A punch to his chiseled jaw feels amazing. Another one to his stomach is cathartic. I don't realize how far gone I am until Holly stops me with a gentle hand on my shoulder.

"He's down," she says softly.

Yes. He's down. Unconscious. Battered and bloody. He's not dead, though, and it would be so easy to twist his neck. More bodies lying in the colonel's wake, and that means more danger to Holly.

I keep him alive.

Not because he deserves it, but because he's more useful if we can threaten him with exposure to take the heat off our backs.

And maybe I keep him alive because I'm done being a killer.

There's a final second of separation and then Holly is in my arms. It feels so good to have her there that I could die now and be happy. But no—I can't die, because Holly is here, and her shoulders are shaking, and she needs me.

I'll live forever. That's what I'll do. I'll live forever so I never have to let her down.

It's only when she tips her face to mine that I see she's not crying. She's shivering, probably from shock and cold, but her eyes are dry. Her hands work over my suit, touching and touching and touching like she doesn't believe I'm here. I barely believe I'm here. She slips one hand around my neck and pulls me down for a kiss. It hurts to be touched but I'll be damned before I let her stop. I'll go all the way to hell and back before I let her stop. I've been there before. I can make it out again.

"You came for me." Her voice trembles with love and I've never heard anything as lovely. Never in my life. There's trust there, trust that I don't deserve but will take as long as she gives it to me. "You came for me, Elijah."

"I'll always come for you, sweetheart."

CHAPTER NINETEEN

ELIJAH

THE LAST TIME I drove Holly to her apartment she was minutes away from being shot.

This time, we take a car and I'm glad for it. Not because I think there will be someone waiting there to shoot her again, though that's always a possibility in this life. But because I can keep her pressed tight against me in the back seat, my arms locked over her. As soon as we pull away from the curb she curls toward the backseat and rests her head on my shoulder.

The driver doesn't say a word.

At the door to her apartment my feet stop working. A threat was on the other side of this door. Part of me will always be in that room, watching her pull the trigger, just like part of me will always be down in the bottom of a well, waiting until it's safe to climb out again.

I can feel her watching me.

"Home sweet home," she says. Her dark eyes

reflect back my own exhaustion and relief.

I wait for her while she takes her key out of her purse and turns it in the lock.

It's obvious as soon as she steps across the threshold that we're not alone.

All the lights are on, like my brother wanted to be sure I'd see him. He stands in Holly's living room, looking for all the world like he's in a business meeting at North Security. He has his phone pressed to his ear, one hand in his pocket. His face says *you're late*.

Holly stops next to me and tosses her purse— a flat, small thing—onto a table by the doorway.

Liam ends his call, his green eyes flashing with relief when he sees us. "What do I have to do to convince you to stop sending yourself on reckless, dangerous, *pointless* missions that are only going to get you killed?"

Heat crawls up the outside of my neck, spurred on by old anger. "There wasn't time to do an extensive risk assessment, Liam. I wasn't sitting on my ass in a cushy leather chair, giving out orders while other people are in the field."

He growls. "If you had kept working for North Security this never would have happened."

"And leave Holly on the run? No, thank you."

Holly steps to my side and puts an arm

around my waist. It hurts even more now that the adrenaline has ebbed away, but I wouldn't stop her for the world.

"The point is," Liam goes on, "you're a loose cannon. Every time you go off on another one of these suicide raids, it makes it harder for me to do what I'm trying to do. What I've finally succeeded in doing, no thanks to you."

"Yes, you made your piles of money all by yourself. Are you here for a reason or just to piss me off? I never asked for a share in North Security. I never asked for a fucking thing from you. Which is just as well, because you taught me what to expect from you early on, when you left. Nothing. Absolutely fucking nothing."

Liam looks like he might strangle me. Well, he's too late. The time for strangling is long past. "I'm trying to tell you that there were other options. I took one of them. I've been in contact with representatives from three other allied countries, and every single one is putting pressure on the government to expose the colonel as a traitor. Once his secrets are out, the senator's won't be far behind. The news breaks tonight."

Tonight has lasted forever, and when he says this, it stops some essential function of my brain. *The news breaks tonight.*

Holly's brain still works.

"Elijah is exonerated?" She takes one tiny step toward Liam, like she can only believe him if she's standing close enough. "We'll both be exonerated? We'll be free?"

"Yes." Liam sighs, and for the first time I can see the toll this has taken on him. He's all serious looks and expensive suits in his regular life. Right now, his face slips into an expression so familiar it makes my chest ache. "All the details have been leaked to the public. There are a few things left to be declassified, but that's happening now. Right now."

I don't know what to say.

My skin doesn't feel like my own skin. My body belongs to someone else. For so many years, I've been running and hiding and putting myself in the darkest corners of the world. I thought I would always stay there. Until Holly, I thought that's where I belonged.

After Holly, I knew there was no way out. Resurfacing was too dangerous for me, and it almost killed her. What Liam is saying now—

It means I could have a life.

A million futures spring into being in front of my eyes. They're wild fantasies, and they only have two things in common: Holly by my side and the oldest possible jealousy.

Through an accident of birth order I was the last one left at home with my father.

Not a day has gone by when I haven't resented my brothers for leaving. And worse—for staying together when I was alone.

Now they all work together in the same place. Meanwhile I'm as unemployed as a person can be. And yes, I do want a vacation. I do want some cottage on a lake with Holly. I do want to hear the reeds in the lake while we lay on the sand.

But I can't be that person forever.

"You have options," Liam says into the cavern of my thoughts. At first he sounds far away, like he's calling down to me from the top of the well. "Take your time with it."

My mouth feels dry. "Options."

"Are you thinking of coming back to North Security?"

"Do you want me to?"

Wanting hits me at the speed of a bullet. It hits all the sensitive parts of me. All the cracks in the armor I've worn all my life. All of it crumbles like weak concrete. It's payback for the years I spent denying that this jealousy and need existed. It's a good thing Holly's standing next to me, because if she weren't, I think I'd fall to my knees on her apartment floor.

I want it so much.

I want it second only to wanting her.

It makes me a different man, a better man, when I work for my brothers. And with them. They're proof positive that a person can climb out of a dark pit and make a life for themselves that's not all mayhem and guilt.

Some mayhem, sure.

That comes with the territory when you work in security.

But there's *more*.

It's pure instinct to deny it to him right now, even with Holly's arm tight around my waist and the question hanging freely between us. *No* is on the tip of my tongue. But Liam didn't ask me if I felt worthy of the job, of my place in the family. In some ways I still don't. In some ways I never will. He asked me if I *wanted* it.

Not just for me, but so that I can be good enough for Holly. She followed her sister to France out of love. She's not the type of woman who wants a life on the run.

"Yes," I tell Liam.

He nods. "Okay. Call me when you're ready to start."

Then he leaves, pausing only to clap me on

the shoulder. It hurts like a motherfucker. It also feels fucking amazing. We aren't exactly huggers. Our family didn't grow up with love and cookies. We had sucker punches and dark wells, but this feels like a start. It feels like a home.

Silence pulls itself over the apartment like a clean sheet. Holly traces the inside of my wrist with her fingertips and takes my hand in hers. The radiator kicks on.

It's the most normal thing I think I've ever experienced with Holly. In another life we could be coming back from a fundraiser that we went to because we wanted to help people, not because she was trying to save me from the clutches of a corrupt government. She'd look just as beautiful in that dress, and I'd look less like a torture victim. It wouldn't hurt to think about taking off my suit jacket. It wouldn't hurt at all.

That other life is like a ghost, visible from the corner of my eye but only real so long as I don't look straight at it.

Another realization dawns, slowly, easily, like a sunrise over a lake.

The ghost life I've never allowed myself to want isn't real *yet*.

It could be real.

Holly killed some of my demons and Liam

just propped open the door to another world.

She squeezes my hand. "Are you okay?"

In some ways it's easier to know that all hope is lost, and any dream you ever have is a survival mechanism meant to keep you from throwing yourself in front of the next available bullet. I've tried that, again and again, and kept on living. Now, to dream and live deliberately, with the whole world in my hands?

It's goddamn terrifying.

I swallow hard and look into Holly's eyes. She's tired, but she still glows, fresh color in her cheeks. It's because of me that she looks that way instead of pale and resigned, the way she was in the parking garage. "Will you marry me?"

In the ghost life I have a ring with an enormous rock and a catered picnic on some French lakeside. In the ghost life I've prepared for this moment for weeks, choosing the perfect day and the perfect moment to ask her. In the ghost life I don't have a half-broken body and I'm not desperate for a bed.

It doesn't matter. Ghost life, this life—I want her in all of them.

Holly's smile chases all the shadows from her face. She lets go of my hand, soft and tentative, and slides both palms up the front of my jacket to my face. She kisses me, the fresh, clean taste of her the only thing I want in every life. "Yes," she says. "I will."

CHAPTER TWENTY
LONDON

WORKING AT THE coffee shop isn't all bad.

For one thing, it leaves me a lot of time outside my head.

I lose myself in the steam wand and hot milk and stirring. The rhythm of brewing and pouring and replacing cups. Sweeping. Replacing fat muffins in the pastry case. It makes it possible, for long stretches of time, to stop thinking about Adam.

He's never far out of mind. It's the internal clock that's slowly ticking me to death.

When I'm at work, my brain eventually quits replaying the night of the fundraiser. It focuses on the drink recipes and the difficult customers and the orders so complicated they should require a degree.

He's been gone for three weeks, four days, and eleven hours.

He never came back after the fundraiser.

I waited up for him.

Not too late, he said. Adam promised me they wouldn't be late, and I believed him. I told Elijah I'd never talk to him again. It was a lie. I knew in my heart that if Adam came back, I would fight with him, and then I'd fuck him, and then we would talk.

I brew a new dark roast and let the thoughts fade into the background. Holly's okay, at least. Elijah came for her, at least. It's right that she has a happy ending while I don't. That fits. She's the *happy ending* sister. I'm the *work as a barista while recovering from a coke habit* sister.

The line stretches out for the morning rush. God bless these caffeine addicts. The morning rush is usually a hectic parade of pissed-off people. Bring them all to me today.

Eventually the crowd thins out, the way it always does. There'll be another rush at lunch with people impatient to get back to the office or trying to extend their break, and then I'll leave, back to the apartment where Adam is not.

There's always a moment when I hesitate before I open the door. It's not that I'm hoping for another catastrophic injury, another emergency Google session. It's more that the couch seems empty without him. The whole space seems empty without him. I take a series of orders from a line of anonymous men and suits. Their faces don't stand out from one another. The last one orders a black coffee. I have two hours left in my shift.

I pump the coffee from the carafe, slide a sleeve onto the cup, and push it back across the counter. "It's one seventy-five," I say, tapping the order into the register.

He drops something onto the counter.

The sound is all wrong for coins.

I take a deep breath and put on a smile, prepared to deliver my jokey yet firm speech about how we don't accept anything but cash or credit for payment. Not bus tokens, not pressed pennies...

...not diamonds.

The words die on my tongue.

Someone has put diamonds on the counter.

I draw my hand back from the coffee cup and look up at his face.

Adam looks different. He's had a haircut and shaved, and that's why I didn't notice him before—he's blending in. He stood in line at the coffee shop like all of those other guys. But he is different, as much as he tries to hide it. The slacks and shirt don't hide anything from me, now that

I'm looking. His overcoat looks expensive. Something he'd wear if he worked for one of the fancy law firms downtown.

Maybe he does. I don't know anything about him now. Not that I knew much before, except—

"It was all for you," he says. "It was always for you."

The door opens and two teenage girls walk in, heads close together, giggling about something. They toss their backpacks into one of the booths along the side of the shop and slide in. It reminds me of me and Holly.

I don't dare touch the diamonds.

"We—" My mouth has gone dry. "We only accept cash and credit for payment."

Adam puts a palm over the diamonds, hiding them from view, and slides them across the counter to me. When he lifts his hand I half-expect the diamonds to be gone. A trick.

They're not a trick.

"I wouldn't leave them out, if I were you."

If there's anything I've learned since I flew to France, it's that touching diamonds is dangerous.

Then again, so is leaving them out on a counter where anyone could walk up and snatch them.

This feels like the moment in the fairy tale just before the girl pricks her finger on the spindle. Before she bites into the poisoned apple. Before the fairy godmother brings her wand down and transforms her into a princess.

"You left," I say. "And you didn't come back. I waited up. For days, I waited up." I take the diamonds in my hands. It's easy enough to slip them into my pocket, out of sight.

Adam reaches into his own pocket and puts a few dollar bills on the counter. "I'm sorry. I was dealing with some shit." He gives a small smile. "Family drama."

I make his change. *Family drama.* That's an understatement. The actions of Lieutenant Colonel Mark Jefferson have been all over the news. Adam's popped up in a few of the articles. He enlisted, like his father and grandfather before him. And he was discharged dishonorably when he tried to bring his father's crimes to light. That decision is being revisited, along with a lot of other shit that's been swept under the carpet for so long.

The diamonds burn a hole in my pocket. I can feel them there, vibrating with possibility and fire, and that's the thing—it feels good.

It feels right.

It feels dangerous and exhilarating and right.

When I look up from the cash register Adam

is at the door. The sight of him on the threshold, about to disappear, turns me into a human scream. I've never unknotted the coffee shop apron so fast in my life.

"Are you leaving?" My coworker, a girl whose name I can never remember, looks at me with wide eyes. She's been in the back doing inventory for the last hour, which is code for playing Animal Crossing on her phone. "It's not the end of your shift yet."

"Yeah, about that—I quit." I lay the apron gently on the counter and sprint for the door.

Adam's tall, with long legs and an even stride, and he's halfway down the block already. I bite back the urge to shout his name. I don't want people watching us right now. What I want— what I want—

I run instead of shouting. I run fast. He pauses at the corner and I put on a burst of speed. I swear to god, if I get there and he's not real, if none of this is real…

My fingers sink into the wool of his coat. His muscles are tensed underneath from holding his coffee cup. He grabbed a lid on the way out.

He smiles and my heart stops.

I can't let go of his sleeve.

"Where are you going?" I sound breathless

and hopeful and slightly scared. "I quit my job."

"Anywhere," he says. "Everywhere. Want to come?"

CHAPTER TWENTY-ONE
ELIJAH

HOLLY IS THINKING.

She does this sometimes, after we've fucked—she just lays there in the bed next to me, her hair spread out on the pillow, looking up at the ceiling with a thoughtful expression.

I can't keep my hands off her.

I trace a path over her collarbone and down her shoulder to the delicate skin of her wrist. "I should leave you alone." Her eyes meet mine, a sharp reply on her lips. "But I won't, because if you tried to run away from me, I'd just kidnap you again."

"Good." Holly laughs, then kisses me, then rolls away. Not far enough that I can't touch her. Just far enough to reach the notebook she keeps on the bedside table. She uncaps her pen with her teeth and props herself up on one elbow to write in it while I absorb myself with the curve of her hip under the sheet. It seems like a shame to leave her skin covered, so I slide the sheet down until it's highlighting her ass. She shivers but keeps writing.

"What is it?"

"What is what?" Her pen moves quickly over the page. I always assumed she wrote everything on a computer, but Holly, I've learned, likes to hand write most of her notes like she's an author from the forties.

"That's a new notebook, isn't it?" She always keeps one close to hand, but this one is green. The color of reeds over water. The old one was a dusky purple.

She twists to look at me over her shoulder, and the grin on her face isn't sheepish or shy. It's proud. "Our story." Holly turns back over and keeps writing.

I don't know how she does it. The story of me and Holly is a long one. All the individual threads of us reach years into the past. There are sisters and brothers and parents. If she wanted the full picture, she'd have to ask her parents about how they got together. Might be a touchy subject. Who knows? This is why she's the writer, not me. "Where does it start?"

"A woman near an ocean," she says absently.

"A mermaid?"

She throws me a look over her shoulder, and honestly, it makes me want to throw the book out the window and fuck her. "Am I a mermaid, Elijah?"

"Maybe." I bite her on the shoulder, and she wriggles against my body, all warm and willing woman, making me hard again. She makes me endlessly hard.

"I'm writing, you know." I bite her again, and Holly twists in my arms and sinks her teeth into my shoulder. "Is this what you wanted?"

Her eyes are bright, wicked, and I pull her on top of me. Holly takes this for the challenge that it is and tries for my wrists. I let her think she's won. I let her pin me so that she can kiss me, her hair falling around our faces like a curtain. She opens her mouth for me and I taste her again, a long stroke of my tongue that makes her forget she's trying to wrestle with me.

Her mistake.

Now *she's* pinned, arms behind her back, both wrists trapped in one of mine. It arches her for me. Holly tips her head back and groans. "This isn't fair."

"What's not fair?" I stroke two fingers between her legs. She's wet there already and sensitive. This isn't the first round of the morning. I push those fingers inside her. "This?"

Her thighs are already shaking. "It's *not* fair," she complains. "I was writing."

"You think you'll write about this?" I'm finger-fucking her now, slow, deliberate strokes. I give her a taste of my thumb on her clit and take it away. This wouldn't be her first orgasm of the morning, either, but she still makes a disappointed noise. "Or this, maybe?"

"No, I wouldn't." She lies through clenched teeth. "I wouldn't write about it unless you stopped being so mean."

"But you like it best this way."

"I don't."

I take my fingers out and circle one of her nipples with her own wetness. "You're not a good liar, sweetheart."

Holly rocks her hips downward, her desperation clear in her red cheeks. "Why are we talking anyway? We could be fucking."

"Good point."

I roll her off me so fast she yelps and bend her over the nearest pillow. It's tied for my favorite position for so many reasons. One of those reasons is that Holly loves it. It makes her red-faced and embarrassed and extremely wet.

She fights me on it because that's what she

always does. It's a game of a protest and I always win.

"Not fair," she pants. "Not fair, Elijah—"

I cover her mouth with my hand, line myself up with her waiting pussy, and thrust home.

The rest of the world does not exist. There's only Holly moaning into my palm and clenching around my cock. Fucking her this way clears my head, and it does something better to Holly. She scrapes her nails down the sheet, trying to reach behind her, and I lean down and pin her wrist to the bed.

She shudders underneath me, a full-body shiver, and her pussy gets hotter. Tighter. Wetter.

One time, in the middle of the night, she woke up from a dead sleep and told me that the white van haunts her dreams. That every time she sees a white van, her heart stutters. And then she pulled *me* on top of *her* and demanded that I pretend.

So I did.

The difference now, obviously, is that there is no white van. It's just me. And whatever fucked-up feelings we both have about all the fucked-up things that happened, it doesn't change the fact that we both have our fantasies.

This is Holly's.

Thank God.

She comes hard, no warning, and opens her mouth to bite the skin between my finger and thumb. I pull my hand back but only so I can turn her face another quarter inch and kiss the side of her lips. "You're mine. My little captive. There's nowhere for you to go, nothing to do but take what I give you, your sweet little cunt wrapped tight around my dick."

"Again," she says.

I put a hand between her legs and haul her closer so I can fuck her harder. This means she has to work for it, angling her hips for maximum contact. When she comes again it's with her face buried in the pillow and both hands clenched into fists. Holly throws her head back, saying something, but I can't make out the words. I'm too lost in the electric tension of taking her. Using her. Wringing out all her orgasms and making her feel mine, too.

Which I do.

It shouldn't be possible to come this hard so many times in one morning, but I manage. I let her have it. I fuck her all the way through. By the time I'm finished with her she's got both hands braced against the headboard. At the bitter end I drop my head down onto her back and rest there until she pushes me away, laughing.

Until she rolls onto her back and throws an arm over her eyes. It takes a while for her breathing to settle, and I indulge myself in the pleasure of watching it.

I think she might fall asleep, but no.

I've barely caught my breath and she's already propped over her notebook again.

"It starts with a woman on a plane." Holly pauses, tapping her pen against her cheekbone. "Maybe it starts before that. The Mona Lisa…." She trails off, scribbling more notes.

"Does it have a name?"

She laughs, a short, musical sound that makes her shoulders shake. "I was thinking of calling it Diamond in the Rough."

"Diamond in the Rough?"

"That's what you are. Diamond in the Rough by Holly Frank. Though it'll have to be sexier than my other stuff. Maybe I'll use a pen name. What do you think?" Holly rolls over onto her back, abandoning the notebook, and threads her arms around my neck.

"Some of that shit is still classified, you know."

"Well," she says, "I can probably change some of the details. It is fiction, after all. To be honest if

I wrote everything as it happened, some people wouldn't believe it."

"Sometimes I don't believe it, and I lived through it."

"We went through all that shit, but there's a silver lining after all. There's this."

My lips quirk in a smile. "A book?"

"No." Her eyes glisten. "You. Us. We're the silver lining."

"I love it," I say, my voice hoarse. "And I love you."

Her eyes melt. Her whole body melts against me. And of course I'm fucking hard again. It never stops with her, and I never want it to. "I love you, too," she whispers.

"Are you going to write that into the book?" Love, I mean.

"Of course. It's the best part."

EPILOGUE
HOLLY

O N OUR FIRST morning in Paris, I wake up to mimosas.

"If you're not walking around Paris drunk on champagne, it's not a honeymoon," Elijah says as he hands me the glass. There's a whole tray of food: croissants and eggs benedict and olives and fruit. He must have ordered the entire breakfast menu.

I laugh without a sound and take a sip of the bubbly orange juice. "What do you know about honeymoons?"

"I know that ours is perfect." He drinks his entire flute of mimosa in one swallow. And then he gives me a small, abashed grin. Even though we're married now, and even though we've been living together for months, it still surprises me to see that expression on his face. No one's smile is more hard-won than Elijah's. "We have a whole city to explore. Where to first?"

I know exactly where I want to go first, and I tell him so.

Elijah shakes his head and laughs. "Do all writers have such an obsession with coming full circle, or is it just you?"

"You don't have to be a writer to appreciate symmetry," I say in a prim voice, though secretly I love when he teases me. Teasing usually turns into something much more fun. But not today—if we have sex all morning, I'll have to nap all afternoon, and this is our honeymoon. We can stay awake all night instead.

An hour later, he keeps his hand on the small of my back in the crowd at the Louvre. Sixteen-year-old me had to keep her feet planted and her elbows out to see the Mona Lisa. She didn't know she was minutes away from meeting the love of her life. All she cared about was finally seeing the most famous painting in the world.

And that was only the beginning.

Now I don't have to keep my elbows out. People just...get out of Elijah's way. He's muscled and large and wears an expression that looks like a scowl even when I know he's pleased. Wherever he's going, a path opens up for him. It's like walking around with my own personal security.

Which he is.

No one blocks our view of the painting this time. I'm a lot closer than I was when I was sixteen. She still looks small—surprisingly small. I still don't know why Da Vinci didn't choose a larger canvas. Something about the size commands my attention. Something about it pulls me in, makes me want to look closer, but the velvet rope stops me.

Elijah leans down and grazes his teeth along the shell of my ear. "Do her eyes follow you?"

"No." This time, when he asks the question, I'm free to turn away from the painting and lean into him. He's warm and solid against my back. And mine. He's mine. "Do they follow you?"

His green eyes twinkle. "Hard to say," he says. "There are more interesting things in the room. She caught my eye years ago in this very spot. I couldn't stop looking at her."

It's so strange and shimmering, standing here with him. I half-expect to see a younger version of myself waiting here with a younger version of him. Me pretending to be cool. Him in his museum security clothes. So much space between us.

"I want to do this," I say.

"This?"

"The tourist stuff. That's what I want to be in

Paris. A tourist. Not someone on the run, with secrets. Not someone with the military closing in. I want to see every sight and go to every tourist trap and buy a bunch of cheesy keychains that cater only to tourists."

"Okay, and we should definitely only speak English."

That one makes me giggle, because Elijah's French is flawless. He can actually tailor his accent as if he were from the north or south, if he's in the upper classes or a working man. He blends in effortlessly here, but it would be funny to see him as the bumbling tourist instead.

We take an Uber to Notre Dame, which wasn't on our visiting list when I came here as a teenager. A hushed sort of quiet greets us as we enter the church. The intricate ceiling and stained glass draw my eyes upward. We've spent a fair amount of time in churches, Elijah and I, but usually in their basements. There are multiple little stands to light candles, and I stop at every single one, dropping in a small donation and selecting a thin, waxy candle.

I didn't come from a religious family, which is ironic. My father was actually a priest before he met my mother, but he fell out of the church, disillusioned and disgraced. Our childhood was loving with easter eggs and warm yuletide traditions, but there was never a sermon to attend on Sundays, never prayers before bedtime. So I'm not even sure I'm doing it right, this prayer thing, but I close my eyes when I light each candle, sending up silent gratitude to whoever looks down on us for keeping Elijah safe, for letting him find his way to me.

We take a photo in front of the Eiffel Tower and marvel together at its size. I'm too crowd averse to take the elevators up, but we do take plenty of photographs. We play with the distance and perspectives, pretending that he's holding the Eiffel Tower on his shoulders, pretending I'm squeezing the whole thing between my thumb and forefinger.

The photos are goofy and out of focus, exactly like they should be for tourists.

They're nothing like the glossy-magazine videos that London takes. She started posting on Instagram again but her TikTok has really taken off. The reveal of her role in the scandal only heightened her celebrity. She has an actual page on Wikipedia now. The good stuff gets posted to social media, but she still sends funny outtakes direct to my phone.

We walk through the shops on Champs-

Élysées and pick up lotions and scarves for outrageous amounts of Euros until my feet hurt so much that Elijah insists on carrying me to the car.

He doesn't let me get out of bed until the next morning.

On the fifth day of our honeymoon I find a new dress on the bed when we come back from an afternoon visiting Sacré-Cœur. "Are you taking me on a date?"

Elijah gives me a mysterious look and turns the next hour into a fun game involving me trying to get ready and him trying to interrupt the process with orgasms. He only stops when a glance at his watch tells him that we're going to be late.

I slap him on the shoulder when the car pulls up in front of a large white building with high arches and an elaborate facade. A crowd of well-dressed people enter the front doors.

"Where are we?"

"The Théâtre de la Ville."

My eyes widen when I take in the poster announcing tonight's presentation. A world class violinist. Samantha Brooks. I've only met her once, at the small civil ceremony that wed Elijah and me. "You didn't tell me your brother was going to be here."

"They had the concert booked a long time ago. Liam was going to leave me alone. He said we didn't have to come, but I told him I could stop fucking you for a couple hours, probably. It will be a hardship, but I'm willing to do it for family."

My cheeks heat. "You did not say that to him."

"Of course I did, though now that I think about it, what's the point of going without? I'm sure we can find a nice quiet, dark place behind some velvet curtains somewhere."

It's not only one of his brothers.

We meet Joshua and Bethany in the third row.

He's wearing a tux. She's wearing a beautiful diaphanous purple gown that makes her look like majesty even sitting down. She gives us a shy wave hello.

Josh smirks at Elijah "I didn't think you two honeymooners were going to make it. Did you get stuck in your hotel room?"

"Shut the fuck up," Elijah tells him good-naturedly. "Where's Liam?"

"Backstage with Samantha." Joshua leans over Elijah, looking like he's about to say something else, but the lights dim before he can. We are at home in this small circle of family. His family. Mine. "Never mind—I'll tell you later."

A single light illuminates the stage, and Samantha Brooks comes out from the wings, ethereal in a silk black dress. She takes her position center stage and bows her head over her violin.

I hold my breath.

The theater falls into a deep, surreal silence. We're all waiting for her to move, for the song to begin. It's the exact feeling I had at sixteen in the moments before I met Elijah.

Stillness, then motion. Silence, then a beginning.

Samantha draws her bow across the strings.

We're not waiting anymore.

The tune she plays is both haunting and romantic, and beside me, Elijah takes a deep breath. He reaches for me without looking. It's a good assumption. I'll always be here, next to him.

I link my fingers with his and hold his hand tight.

THE END

Thank you for reading SILVER LINING! There's a free bonus epilogue, too. Make sure you're signed up for the VIP Reader list so you get it in your inbox:

www.skyewarren.com/silver-epilogue

And if you loved the North brothers, read Liam North's story now!

Forbidden fruit never tasted this sweet…

> "Swoon-worthy, forbidden, and sexy, Liam North is my new obsession."
>
> – New York Times bestselling author
> Claire Contreras

The world knows Samantha Brooks as the violin prodigy. She guards her secret truth—the desire she harbors for her guardian.

Liam North got custody of her six years ago. She's all grown up now, but he still treats her like a child. No matter how much he wants her.

No matter how bad he aches for one taste.

The middle North brother Joshua also has a book!

Blood and sweat. Bethany Lewis danced her way out of poverty. She's a world class athlete... with a debt to pay.

Joshua North always gets what he wants. And the mercenary wants Bethany in his bed. He wants her beautiful little body bent to his will.

She doesn't surrender to his kiss.

He doesn't back down from a challenge.

It's going to be a sensual fight... to the death.

AUDITION is an emotional second chance romance!

Keep reading for an excerpt from OVERTURE...

✧　✧　✧

REST, LIAM TOLD me.

He's right about a lot of things. Maybe he's right about this. I climb onto the cool pink sheets, hoping that a nap will suddenly make me content with this quiet little life.

Even though I know it won't.

Besides, I'm too wired to actually sleep. The white lace coverlet is both delicate and comfy. It's actually what I would have picked out for myself, except I didn't pick it out. I've been incapable of picking anything, of choosing anything, of deciding anything as part of some deep-seated fear that I'll be abandoned.

The coverlet, like everything else in my life, simply appeared.

And the person responsible for its appearance? Liam North.

I climb under the blanket and stare at the ceiling. My body feels overly warm, but it still feels good to be tucked into the blankets. The blankets *he* picked out for me.

It's really so wrong to think of him in a sexual way. He's my guardian, literally. Legally. And he has never done anything to make me think he sees *me* in a sexual way.

This is it. This is the answer.

I don't need to go skinny-dipping in the lake down the hill. Thinking about Liam North in a sexual way is my fast car. My parachute out of a plane.

My eyes squeeze shut.

That's all it takes to see Liam's stern expression, those fathomless green eyes and the glint of dark blond whiskers that are always there by late afternoon. And then there's the way he touched me. My forehead, sure, but it's more than he's done before. That broad palm on my sensitive skin.

My thighs press together. They want something between them, and I give them a pillow. Even the way I masturbate is small and timid, never making a sound, barely moving at all, but I can't change it now. I can't moan or throw back my head even for the sake of rebellion.

But I can push my hips against the pillow, rocking my whole body as I imagine Liam doing more than touching my forehead. He would trail his hand down my cheek, my neck, my shoulder.

Repressed. I'm so repressed it's hard to imagine more than that.

I make myself do it, make myself trail my hand down between my breasts, where it's warm and velvety soft, where I imagine Liam would know exactly how to touch me.

You're so beautiful, he would say. *Your breasts are perfect.*

Because Imaginary Liam wouldn't care about big breasts. He would like them small and soft with pale nipples. That would be the absolute perfect pair of breasts for him.

And he would probably do something obscene and rude. Like lick them.

My hips press against the pillow, almost pushing it down to the mattress, rocking and rocking. There's not anything sexy or graceful about what I'm doing. It's pure instinct. Pure need.

The beginning of a climax wraps itself around me. Claws sink into my skin. There's almost certain death, and I'm fighting, fighting, fighting for it with the pillow clenched hard.

"Oh fuck."

The words come soft enough someone else might not hear them. They're more exhalation of breath, the consonants a faint break in the sound. I have excellent hearing. Ridiculous, crazy good hearing that had me tuning instruments before I could ride a bike.

My eyes snap open, and there's Liam, standing there, frozen. Those green eyes locked on mine. His body clenched tight only three feet away from me. He doesn't come closer, but he doesn't leave.

Orgasm breaks me apart, and I cry out in surprise and denial and relief. "*Liam.*"

It goes on and on, the terrible pleasure of it. The wrenching embarrassment of coming while looking into the eyes of the man who raised me for the past six years.

My hips pump against the mattress, pulling out the last few pulses between my legs.

And then I'm lying there, wrapped tight around a pillow, unable to move, panting.

I've never seen Liam looking anything other than calm and cool and capable. He can handle anything with a command that's almost terrifying in its competency. Right now he looks at a loss.

His voice is low and rough. "We should talk about this."

I can't think of anything in the world I'd rather do less. "Or we could just…" I hate that I still somehow sound breathy and turned on. There are little quivers in my thighs. "Pretend this never happened?"

"Come downstairs when you're—"

The sentence hangs between us, leaving me to fill in the blank. *Come downstairs when you're done fucking yourself in the bed I bought for you. Come downstairs when you're done humiliating yourself.*

He gives a short nod, as if the unspoken answer is the right one.

Then he turns, an about-face appropriate to any military ceremony.

Alone in the room I have no choice but to face the mechanics of untangling myself. Unclenching my fists from the pillow. Pulling apart my legs. Acknowledging the dampness between my thighs.

"Please be a dream," I whisper, but my face is too hot. Burning up. This is real.

Want to read more? Order OVERTURE from Amazon, Barnes & Noble, Apple Books, or Kobo.

BOOKS BY SKYE WARREN

Secret

Sweet

Deep

Stripped series

Tough Love

Love the Way You Lie

Better When It Hurts

Even Better

Pretty When You Cry

Caught for Christmas

Hold You Against Me

To the Ends of the Earth

Standalone Dangerous Romance

Wanderlust

On the Way Home

Hear Me

**For a complete listing of Skye Warren books,
visit
www.skyewarren.com/books**

About the Author

Skye Warren is the New York Times bestselling author of dangerous romance such as the Endgame trilogy. Her books have been featured in Jezebel, Buzzfeed, USA Today Happily Ever After, Glamour, and Elle Magazine. She makes her home in Texas with her loving family, sweet dogs, and evil cat.

Sign up for Skye's newsletter:
www.skyewarren.com/newsletter

Like Skye Warren on Facebook:
facebook.com/skyewarren

Join Skye Warren's Dark Room reader group:
skyewarren.com/darkroom

Follow Skye Warren on Instagram:
instagram.com/skyewarrenbooks

Visit Skye's website for her current booklist:
www.skyewarren.com

COPYRIGHT

This is a work of fiction. Any resemblance to actual persons, living or dead, business establishments, events or locales is entirely coincidental. All rights reserved. Except for use in a review, the reproduction or use of this work in any part is forbidden without the express written permission of the author.

Printed in Great Britain
by Amazon

62508845R00135